THE SWINDLERS AND THE SQUALL

JOSEPH PARADIS

Cover design and interior
www.ebooklaunch.com

Edited by Mike Waitz of Sticks and Stones Freelance Editing
www.stickandstonesediting.net

Author Website
www.AeneriaIsComing.com

FROM THE WORLD OF AENERIA

<u>Saving the Dark Side</u>

Book 1: The Devotion

Book 2: The Harbingers

Book 3: The Unbound

<u>The Swindlers and The Squall</u>

Her Gift, for You

For all Hate mail and love letters:
www.AeneriaIsComing.com/contact/

This book is for those callous few with true Hunger in their hearts, and those brave souls who dare love with all their Passion.

CHAPTER 1

STEALING IN

"May you rot in there till the end of your days, you thievin' rat," the jailer spat through the bars. His gritty fingers twisted the lock on the cell door, clicking it shut. "Hope you enjoyed that little bite you stole. Hope it filled you right up. It'll be the last meal you ever have."

The jailer patted his rotund belly, jiggling the naked girth that hung below his shirt. The man wore the crest of the Galdebrean Army on his chest, but judging by his perpetual sweating and panting, his soldiering days were long behind him.

"What do you mean it's my last meal?" Varka asked, gripping the bars. "Do the Galdebrean courts execute men for taking a bit of food? Will there be no trial?"

"Of course there's gonna be a trial!" The jailer rapped the bars with an iron-banded club, nearly cleaving Varka's fingers. Chuckling, he brought the tip of the club to his cheek, scratching it against his stubble. "I 'spect your trial will take place in a few months. Maybe two, if I book you this week. Only I don't feed criminals. No need to be spendin' taxpayer money on thieves. How long do you think you can go without food anyhow?"

"I think the smell will do me in first, if we're being honest with each other, Jamarkus," Varka said, pulling at the shackles on his wrists. "I don't suppose I could get you to remove these? If I'm to starve to death then at least grant me use of my hands. It's not as if I'm going anywhere anytime soon."

Jamarkus slapped the club against the bars once more, this time producing a shower of sparks. "Sense of humor eh? We'll see how funny you think you are after a few days with nothin' but your own body to feed on. Who knows, maybe I'll let Rhed join you. Keep you company." Jamarkus pointed a thumb over his shoulder to a wiry figure clinging to the bars a few cells down. "Ol' Rhed's been down here for a whole cycle now. Been sustainin' himself on the bodies of those who starve first. Sometimes he don't wait that long though. Sometimes he gets too hungry. Starts on em while they're still squirmin'."

"Charming," Varka remarked, openly disgusted at the man called Rhed, who was currently reaching a skinny arm at him through the bars. The man looked like a living skeleton. He wore nothing but a soiled rag tied around his waist and his skin was littered with weeping sores.

"Not so clever now, are ya, thief?" Jamarkus sneered. "How'd you learn my name anyhow? Answer me and I'll wait an extra day before lettin' Rhed out to meet you."

Cocking his head, Varka inspected Jamarkus from his greasy, balding head to his tattered leather boots. Varka didn't like lying to honest men, but the fat jailer was neither an honest or decent man. A little lie would do just nicely here, and the oaf would probably eat it right up, just as he had been eating the rations meant for the prisoners.

Varka offered the lie on an offhanded tone, "The soldier that put me in your charge called you by name."

Eyes darkening, Jamarkus pulled his pants up a little higher. "A thief *and* a liar eh?" He turned, waddling back down the row of cells towards the exit. "Hope you're hungry, Rhed. Got a real *fresh* one here for you."

Rhed's frantic breath rushed in and out through his bared teeth, which had been filed to points. He stretched both arms through the bars, moaning like a child as his black nails groped at the air between him and Varka.

"Nah, not now Rhed." Jamarkus tapped his club against the cell frame. "He's a bit too lively. Best wait a few days or he'll snap your bones like kindlin'. Here, gnaw on this for now." Chubby fingers dove into a shallow pocket at the jailer's belt. The remnants of Varka's stolen roast were chewed down to the bone and cartilage. Jamarkus flicked the lump through the bars. Rhed inspected it, picking it up with the tips of his spindly fingers as if appraising a precious gem. "That'll hold you over for now, Rhed. Just don't go chokin' on it."

A ring of keys jingled at Jamarkus's belt as he shoved one into Rhed's lock, opening his cell door. Rhed showed no interest whatsoever as he started on the hunk of meat. Jamarkus glanced back at Varka, flashing him a yellow-toothed grin before waddling towards the stairs, whistling a sailor's tune all the while. The cell block door clanged shut as the whistling slowly faded away.

Varka waited a moment, ignoring the slurping coming from Rhed's now open cell. His eyes traced along the wet stone ceiling, looking through to where he knew Jamarkus to be. As Varka knew from his brief observations of the jailer, his confiscated valuables were now being squirreled away into a vault on the second floor. A few meager effects; an embroidered leather purse full of masterfully counterfeited coins, a hand-drawn map of Galdebreah, and most importantly, Varka's enchanted necklace. No matter how far the greedy jailer took the necklace, Varka would know exactly where to find it.

Unlike the ox lumbering about upstairs, Varka was a man of magic. He was born in a river town far from Galdebreah, where magic didn't merely flit about campfire stories. Varka was from the Dark Side of Aeneria, where magic permeated everything from the air to the very soil they walked on. Varka came from a line of capable magic-users who'd taught him the secrets of Aeneria. While tragedy had cut Varka's education short, he was still leagues ahead of anyone on the light side, especially Jamarkus.

When Varka no longer felt his necklace moving about, he waited another few minutes. He couldn't sense the jailer's location, but it was safe to assume he'd be back at his desk by now, enjoying the rations of dead prisoners.

As his mother had taught him, Varka shut out all thought and cast aside his emotions. Emotions clouded one's view of the world and had no purpose for users of Wisdom. While he didn't agree with a life of cold logic, Wisdom was useful at the moment, so he called it to his aid.

A wire of emerald light shot from Varka's finger, snaking its way down his hand and into the lock on his shackles. With a smirk, the heavy iron clicked open and fell to the stone floor with a clunk. There was a pause in the chewing coming from Rhed's cell. Varka waited for the cannibal to resume his gnawing before undoing the lock on his own cell, quietly this time. Once his door was free, he snatched his shackles from the wet floor.

Shafts of daylight pierced through cutouts in some of the cells, filling the cell block with beams of rusty light while leaving certain portions bathed in darkness. Varka ran a glowing palm along the frame of his cell door, muffling the dried hinges with another spell. He pushed the cold iron of his cell door, which glided open without a sound. Exiting his cell, Varka convinced the surrounding darkness onto himself until he couldn't see his own feet. To old Rhed he would appear as nothing more than a passing shadow.

Avoiding the shafts of light, Varka crept through the block, pausing to get a better look at the cannibal. Cloaked in his magic, Varka tugged Rhed's cell door a little wider, producing a metallic screech. Rhed perked up, clenching a bone between his filed teeth. His empty eyes gazed through Varka, then to the open door. Like a cautious animal, Rhed shuffled out of his cell and into Varka's.

Varka hefted his iron shackles and made his way up the stairs, leaving the cannibal to wander free in search of his next meal. He placed a spell over his cuffs before setting them on the top step. Holding his breath, he knocked three times on the heavy oak door.

"Damn you Rhed, I just sat down!" Jamarkus shouted from behind the door. It sounded as if he spoke through a mouthful of food.

Varka pulled more shadows over himself, holding his breath. He peered under the crack of the door as he saw the jailer's boots shuffle over. Keys jingled and the door swung open, soaking Varka in plain daylight. It took all of his focus to maintain the shadows with his Wisdom.

"What's this then?" Jamarkus groaned as he placed a hand on his knee, squatting to pick up Varka's manacles.

Varka's trap spell ignited with the prodding of the jailer's fingers. The iron cuffs sprang to life and crawled spider-like up his hand. With a loud snap, the manacle secured itself on the jailer's wrist. Panicking, Jamarkus yanked at the iron with his free hand, only to squeal in terror as the device clamped around it.

Unable to maintain the Wisdom any longer, Varka shed his shadows and dove around Jamarkus. To his dismay he found himself pinned between the door frame and the jailer's bulbous girth.

"What in bloody hell!" Jamarkus's neck wobbled as his eyes went wide. "I don't think so laddie!"

Varka gasped as Jamarkus pressed his body into him. He struggled with all his might, but the jailer was more than twice his size and incredibly dense. He was thoroughly stuck. Jamarkus threw an elbow into Varka's ribs, driving the air from his lungs. The blow enticed another type of magic from deep within Varka. The red magic begged to come off its leash.

No, he couldn't. He mustn't. The red magic was too wild, too risky, even for this. Desperation mixing with creativity, Varka cast a hasty spell at the jailer's feet, rendering them slick and gripless. Jamarkus wobbled and Varka freed himself, but not before snatching a ring of keys from the jailer's belt. Before Jamarkus could call for help, Varka allowed the red magic just a little slack. He kicked the jailer square in the gut, sending him careening through the air and down the stone steps. The fall likely wouldn't kill him, though the hungry cannibal might.

Varka slammed the door shut, locking it with Jamarkus's keys. Gasping with his hands on his knees, Varka took a moment to catch his breath and settle the red magic before it burned any hotter. Once composed, he shook himself straight and started up another flight of stairs. As he followed the magical anchor to his necklace, a sickening question bubbled to the fore of his mind. Did he just kill a man? He shook the question away. Now was not the time to think on it.

Varka's necklace pulled him up to the third floor, where he found an office full of stacked cabinets and shelves. Piled here and there were crusty ledgers and messy stacks of files displaying names of long dead prisoners. There was a silty layer of dust over every surface, save for a worn path leading to a peculiar mauve carpet in the corner.

Keeping his feet on the worn path, Varka crossed the room and peeled back the carpet. Embedded in the wooden floor was a heavy safe. The jailer's greasy fingerprints and crumbs littered the entire thing. Varka considered cutting through the safe with magic. It would be quicker, but sloppy. No, he wouldn't make a mess on Jamarkus's account. He would crack it the hard way and do the job properly.

Calling his Wisdom to his fingertips, he deposited a glowing emerald bead into an ear before pressing his head flat against the face of the safe. The magic tickled like an icy insect, as it sharpened his hearing far beyond its ordinary limits. He could hear every little gear and cam within the lock as he twisted it, ticking and dancing around the dial like a mechanical symphony. Following the satisfying drum of the combination gears, the safe yielded to him with a satisfying clunk.

Varka pried the heavy door open, revealing a small mountain of treasures glinting through the dusty air. He recognized fat sapphires and peridots, hulking topazes and rubies, all buried within a knotted mess of silver and gold. It was almost too much to carry.

Pockets sagging, Varka donned his enchanted necklace and made for the exit, wiping all trace of his presence with the magic of Wisdom. He came back to the front office, which was deathly quiet. He pressed his Wisdom-augmented ear to the door, listening for a struggle. His heart thumped with cold blood. There was only silence.

Instead of checking on Jamarkus, he looked to the ledger set on the jailer's desk. The ledger was too neat, too clean. The records indicated dozens of prisoners moving in and out of the jail every month, each awaiting trial for no longer than a week. To his superiors, Jamarkus would be seen as doing the workload of two or three wardens. Like himself, Jamarkus was a thief. Unlike himself, Jamarkus took more than the honest swindler's share. The cannibal in the basement was testament to that fact. While he was not entirely at ease with his unintended murder, the evidence in the ledger would allow him to sleep without regret.

With a small fortune jangling in his pockets, Varka departed the jail through the front door. The streets were bustling with screaming youths and wagons piled high with goods coming in and out of the port. No one noticed or cared about a lone man strolling out of the district jail.

Chapter 2

Ecstasy

Every city on Aeneria's Light Side had its networks of thieves and black markets. Each had strict rules to live and work under. An offense among any of the guilds yielded a hefty price that few thieves could afford. A quiet death awaited anyone who took more than his share, or stole from the wrong party. The swift justice of the black market resulted in an ecosystem of thieves who all abided by the whims of their local guilds. Rules existed for good reason and were followed by all. All except for Varka.

As the citizens of Aeneria's Light Side were ignorant of all magic, Varka had made a fruitful career for himself as a master thief. Shadows bent for him, dice danced for him, and trinkets leaped from their owners' pockets into his own. As far as thieves went, Varka didn't consider himself a bad person. He never stole more than his targets could afford to lose, and his wealth usually found its way into the hands of those who needed it. His favorite victims were other thieves who took more than the honest swindler's share. After cycles of lifting jewelry from nobles and cheating cheaters at card tables, Varka had grown tired of the usual fair. He'd set his sights on bigger game, each haul fatter than the last. It was not uncommon for him to take in a year's salary in a single night's work. As the guilds and black market had no way of detecting Varka's meddling, there was simply no stopping him. As his eye for treasure grew, so did his wanderlust. After he cashed the purse from the prison job, Varka would set sail on the most tremendous heist of his career.

Varka exchanged his stolen jewels with a top-tier fence before making his way to the Galdebrean docks. He carried a bulging wallet of the local currency; however, most of his wealth rested in credit with the black markets. As a result, he received special treatment among guild-sponsored establishments. Seeing as every hotel, bar, and shop was owned by one guild or another, Varka hardly ever paid for anything in the cities he worked in.

The Galdebrean Docks were certainly not the wealthiest district in the city, but there was something in the port that would make Varka richer than any other. Tonight was a special night for not only Galdebreah, but all of Aeneria. Tonight the sun would set proper, bringing Aeneria from the house of Balmoray to the house of Shaskein. Galdebreah exalted in the passing of every local planet with wanton celebration. The merriment spilled into the streets as the city immolated itself with a lust for life. It was the perfect night for a master thief.

Dressed in his finest clothes, Varka wove through the port-district slums on his way to his next job. He stood out like a flower in a dung pile, ignoring the greedy eyes and hungry hands that followed. Aenerians with more nefarious dispositions saw Varka as a lost nobleman, and were all too eager to lighten the burdens in his pockets. Blind to magic, the would-be thieves found themselves tripping over loose cobblestones, or clubbed over the head by falling shop signs.

After an uneventful stroll aided by his Wisdom, Varka rounded the final corner and set his eyes on his target. Waves sloshed against the docks, which were full of elegant party boats taking on passengers. Groups of nobles boarded the vessels accompanied by their own security escort. Varka recognized a few of the guards from the local guilds, no doubt making a dishonest profit while doing honest work. There were yachts and barges crammed along the lengths of the docks, each decorated and stocked for a night of celebration. Varka appraised each ship as he walked by. A clever thief could make a fortune with so many drunken aristocrats all packed together like this. On a typical night any of the ships he passed by would have been worthy of his craft, but this was not a typical night. Tonight, he set his sights on the Ecstasy.

The Ecstasy lay on a private dock, bobbing lightly in the ocean breeze as if in invitation. She was rumored to have been crafted by engineers from Aeneria's Dark Side, where wizards had lined her hull with spells and laced her sails with enchantments. She was reputed as the fastest ship on the ocean, as well as the most luxurious. Rumors of her extravagance and beauty were of little concern to Varka. What piqued his interest was a secret known only to two people: The Ecstasy could be crewed by one man. Varka intended to be that man.

A portly man wearing a captain's tricorn and a sweeping moustache waved nobles along the Ecstasy's gangway. "Step on up my ladies and lords. Hold out your vouchers and the staff will check you off. Your personal effects will be waiting in your rooms, safe and sound. Step on up now."

Varka straightened his collar and packed himself into the eager throng funneling onto the gangway. He took a quick inventory of his fellow passengers, relieved that his attire matched their elegant dresses and crisp suits. A gap opened in the crowd, giving him a close view of the Ecstasy for the first time. Her hull was painted a pale blue, complemented by the rich auburn woodwork that embellished the vessel in exotic patterns. Sweeping balustrades wandered up and down her decks, drawing the eyes to distant fountains and statues. She was a rare beauty indeed.

"Travelling stag are we?" The captain held out his hand, flashing Varka a look of mock reprisal. "No one travels the seas alone, save for the rascals and cheaters. Which might you be then?"

"Depends, on if I'm gambling or in the company of a bold woman," Varka quipped, offering the captain his voucher. "I was told the Ecstasy offered both."

"An honest swindler!" The captain chuckled. He held his belly as he laughed, as though keeping his girth from shaking the buttons off his blazer. "I'd give you the most comfortable cell in the brig, if we had one that is," he added in a wheezing laugh.

"I'd settle for a drink with the captain," Varka said, setting his voucher in the captain's hand. He dropped his voice to a loud whisper, "I may have smuggled a bottle of seven-cycle Scamorhorn in my luggage. The port authorities frown on Dark Side imports, but for an occasion such as this, well I couldn't resist."

"Oho! And good taste to boot!" The captain returned Varka's mischievous smile with a bushy grin of his own. "Don't you worry my good man, fineries of the Dark Side are appreciated aboard this vessel, I assure you." He slid his hand along a polished bannister. "The Ecstasy was born on the Dark Side, you know. There are few things a man can resist once in her embrace."

"That's why I came," Varka replied.

Once aboard, Varka donned an appropriate visage of curiosity, admiring every inch of the Ecstasy while touring various decks. The crew were all too willing to bring him behind closed doors, showing him the inner workings of the facilities and riggings. A senior crewmember even brought him up to the helm, boasting over the advanced technology and dropping heavy hints of the ship's enchantments.

The Ecstasy disembarked with a trumpeting blast from a brass horn above the helm. The passengers rushed to the sides, eager to see the ship's magic first hand. Varka thought it odd that the nobles of the Light Side took such interest, as none of them would openly admit they believed in such fairy tales. Yet here they were, shoving and scratching at each other like animals to get a view of the hull, which was now floating several feet above the water. The black-velvet sails pulled themselves tight without the aid of wind. They were properly off, gliding above the water without the slightest chattering from the waves below.

The other passengers wasted no time delving into their vices. The crew worked like a well-oiled machine, flitting about wherever empty glasses or growling stomachs appeared. Troubadours emerged from nowhere, covering every deck of the ship so no ear was without music. Varka grudgingly fell prey to the song and mirth, indulging himself in a dance here, a drink there. He may have been on a job, but that was no reason not to enjoy himself. After the sun set he would be very much alone for the foreseeable future.

Somewhere in the blur he found himself locked in a dance with a woman whose charms were as captivating as they were deadly. The thief in him told him to keep his distance, to protect his pockets. However, the man in him threw his reservations overboard, feasting on her wandering hands and her supple qualities as they danced in close embrace. All too soon the song was over, and so was the dance. Varka regretted not getting her name, but it wouldn't matter in a few hours anyhow. He would remember her eyes though. They were the same pale blue as the Ecstasy's hull. Her wild auburn hair even matched the ship's elegant woodwork. He noted a familiar scent about her too, as if she carried a fragrance that reminded him of home.

Varka meandered through the crowds, sampling the cavalcade of nobles aboard. He had little in common with the lords and ladies of Aeneria's Light Side, but perhaps one day he could. Varka had enough money set aside where he could join their circles and start a new life. He often fantasized about abandoning his life of solitude and settling into the trappings of an honest living. Varka sighed, joining a group who invited him to watch the sunset from the top deck. He would live his fantasy of normalcy, if only for tonight.

The sails were furled as the Ecstasy turned broadside to the ever-shrinking city of Galdebreah. Balmoray's star hung just out of sight, below the horizon of the coastal city. The star painted the wispy clouds in brilliant scarlets and deep magentas. The city's skyline stood as an inky silhouette, giving the city an appearance of a black forest reaching for the heavens.

On the horizon opposite, the planet Balmoray glinted its farewell. The planet stood out in the darkened sky like a bowl of swirling blue and white fire. Rainbow clouds bloomed through Aeneria's uppermost atmospheres, rushing to the local planet. Varka's upbringing taught him that the clouds were soul flies, mysterious animals of pure energy hurrying back home before Aeneria faded into the aethers. With a quiet grin, he listened to the braggadocious explanations from the men of the upper deck, each spinning a different mundane tale for the colorful anomaly.

Balmoray's star pulsed below the city skyline, eliciting cheerful cries from the passengers. With a final flash, the star and the local planet vanished, leaving the sky in darkness absolute. Silence fell over the ship as each passenger found a set of lips for the customary farewell kiss. Varka gazed up at the empty sky, counting the new stars as they sparked to life. Aeneria was now in the house of Shaskein. The cloudy green planet shimmered into existence directly above the Ecstasy, provoking a roar of welcome from the deck.

Varka wove through the crowds of revelers, indulging himself in a few more hours of a normal life. He drank more than he'd intended, eventually finding himself below deck in a gambling parlor. He certainly didn't need the money, but Varka couldn't resist an opportunity to lighten the purses of the fortunate. He settled himself into a game of cards at a table full of business moguls. Varka encouraged the gamblers by losing most hands; however, he marked each card with Wisdom unseen by the others.

"The stars shine on me tonight!" cried a reedy man in a striped suit as he pounded the table. Coins fell from neat stacks as the dealer scooped the man his winnings. "Don't worry Varney, you'll get yours soon enough," he chuckled at Varka.

Varka considered the man, declining to correct him on his name. He addressed the table, pulling more coin from deeper in his pockets, "What I lose in money I gain in humility, though at this rate I'll have the modesty of a saint by the end of the night."

Hearty laughter erupted around the table as a servant carted in more drinks. The reedy man clapped Varka on the back, foisting a tall bottle into his hands. "For the gracious loser. If you're going to lose to the best then it's only right you drink with the best! Come now boys, to Varney's good luck!"

Bottles clinked as the table cheered to Varka's good fortune. Varka returned the gesture with a reserved smile, throwing the bottle back. The next hand came out and Varka feigned a look of frustration. "Seas take me, I've learned enough for the night. If one of you gentlemen would be so kind as to knock me out this round, I'll put all in." Varka shoved his remaining coin into the center of the table. Three men folded, but three others matched his bet, including the man who'd bought him a drink.

"Your patience is what's killing you here Varney," laughed the man in the striped suit as he counted out his coins, throwing the last one into the pool. "But that's the downfall of the young stag isn't it? First to charge, but first to fall to the wisdom of the older bucks."

"Wisdom indeed," Varka replied with a polite grin.

A tense moment later, the dealer flipped the final card of the match, eliciting grumbles of dissent around the table. He closed his gaping mouth, shaking himself. "Um, this round goes to Varney."

Now coinless, the three losers took their leave. The remaining men looked at Varka with newfound respect, as if a predator had just come into their midst. Varka stacked his winnings, excusing his victory as beginner's luck and buying them all a round. Reassured, the men settled deeper into their drink, putting the thirst back in their eyes.

The parlor door swung open, drawing the eyes of everyone in the room. Varka kept his head down, but noted a familiar scent wafting into the room. He didn't need to look up to know who just sidled up in the chair next to him.

The dealer loosened his collar. "These seats are for gamblers only, miss. Do you intend to play?"

A sheet of auburn hair fell over the table as she leaned closer, revealing inviting features through her low-cut lace. "Only if one of you brutes would be so kind as to teach me." Even from his periphery Varka could feel her pale blue eyes calling to him.

In unison, the three gamblers opposite Varka chimed in, offering tips, strategy, and small mountains of coin. Varka remained quiet, never bringing his eyes too close to her. There was something odd to this woman.

"Why thank you boys!" Her voice was rich and mature. Varka found it increasingly difficult not to look at her. "I hope your generosity extends to the match as well. Best of luck to us all!"

The men each made their unintelligible grumbles of response. Varka felt a shift in the air, but he couldn't put a fine enough point to it. He shook himself, dismissing his suspicions. Probably just the liquor and gentle rocking of the Ecstasy.

"Good luck indeed!" The dealer chuffed, shuffling the cards with a flourish that he had yet to display. "Hands up and bets down. Cards on the table." In a practiced motion, he flung them their hands, placing the common cards face down in the center.

Something squeezed Varka's upper-arm.

"My memory's terrible, what do we do first?" Her breath caressed the side of his face as she whispered. Her hand lingered on his arm.

Varka nearly dropped the spells he'd placed on the deck. Taking a steadying breath, he braved her eyes. They were far more striking than he remembered. "Just watch the others, sweet one. You seem a crafty woman. You'll pick things up in a match or two. It's not like you're gambling with your own money."

She drew herself even closer so that only Varka could hear. Her body pressed gently into his. "I gamble with many things, but never with my own money."

"Like I said, crafty," Varka replied, forcing his head away. He took a deep pull from his drink. Her pale blues were still on him.

"First-mountain's closed. Valley bets are open," the dealer tapped the front of the common pile.

Varka saw the greed in the men's eyes, each eager to impress the blue-eyed woman. With barely a look at their hands, they each thrust their whole stack of coins to the valley-circle. This was exactly what Varka had hoped for. He double checked his markings on the cards before sliding his entire stack in as well.

With a series of sharp snaps, the dealer's nimble fingers revealed the rest of the common cards. Varka was already counting his winnings when something caught his eye. One of the common cards was naked, completely devoid of his magical mark. Trepidation bloomed in Varka's gut as the dealer worked his way closer to the suspicious card.

Slamming fists and curses erupted from the table, Varka included. The only person unaffected was the blue-eyed woman.

With a cautious glance to either side, the dealer waited for a lull in the collective tirade before making his announcement. "This round goes to…Miss?"

"Everbeam," the woman replied, blinking and apparently befuddled. "But what just happened? Did I lose?"

The dealer took a breath, running a hand through his hair as he searched for the words. One of the gamblers across the table answered first, however.

"You just cleaned out the whole damned table!" he shouted, standing so fast that his chair clattered to the floor. "Ever since Varney stepped in the whole game's been off-kilter. Luck be damned, I'm done for the night. May you choke on the winnings, Miss Everbeam."

The men gathered their drinks and left, making as much noise as possible on the way out. Varka rose, slowly pushing his chair back in. How could he have missed a card? He was quite sure he'd marked them all. In the end he chalked it up to the liquor, not to mention the distraction of the biggest heist of his career. Making his excuses, he finished his drink and followed after the other losers. As he closed the door he chanced a final glimpse at Miss Everbeam. Through the gaps in her auburn hair a pale-blue eye and a sly grin watched him leave the parlor.

CHAPTER 3

SOME FLOWERS HAVE THORNS

Varka descended to the belly of the Ecstasy. Something very important waited for him in his cabin. He lit a single flickering lamp and secured the latch on his door. He then further locked it with a spell, swelling the door into the frame. He found his bags were waiting for him on his bed, right where the captain had said they'd be. He opened the biggest case first. A heap of nobleman's clothes looked back up at him, all colorful and none comfortable. He closed the case and ran his hand down a hidden latch along the spine. He threw the lid open once more and the case revealed his true possessions.

Varka tore off his formal clothes and pulled out a silky, flowing material which looked like liquid smoke; his shadow suit. The hooded garment was form-fitting, yet stretched in all the right places. Most importantly it was woven with Wisdom. The suit allowed Varka to move without making a sound, even if he should cast himself down a flight of stairs.

Next, Varka pulled a bandoleer from the case, wrapping it tightly across his chest and back. The item itself was not magical, but it had enough pockets and straps wherein a clever thief could store a small warehouse of magical objects. Varka patted the bandoleer, ensuring none of its content would come loose during transport.

Donning his gloves and padded shoes, he looked himself once over in a standing mirror, ensuring nothing was out of place. The liquor still buzzed merrily in his head, but it was easy enough to convince himself that he'd do just fine. Even if he should make some fatal blunder and reveal himself, there was little that could be done to stop him. His Wisdom would take care of him as it always had. And if by some rare misfortune the green magic was not enough, then the red magic would tend to him. Varka hadn't a name for the red magic. He only knew the power it gave him, and the cost for using it. The terrible magic had only revealed its full power to him once before, and he had no intention of calling it again.

Shaking away the memories, Varka left his cabin and secured the latch without a sound. He pulled the shadows close and made for the top deck, ready to start the first phase of the heist.

The upper decks bustled with revelers, each reaching a level of carefree drunk that only rich nobles on holiday could achieve. Doctors, executives, professors, all finally free of the trappings of their day to day. Varka watched from above as the variety of aristocrats melded into a stew of debauchery. The passengers were so engrossed, Varka was quite sure he could execute this part naked without rousing suspicion. The whole spectrum of Galdebrean upper-class had degenerated to a riot of drunkards.

After witnessing a hair-yanking scuffle between two women clad in jewelry, Varka was grateful he'd taken the stealthy approach. He watched from above the party lights as a bartender casually waved to a tinted glass window across the patio. Three men in plain clothes appeared from nowhere and separated the thrashing women, silencing them with quick blows to the neck. None of the other guests noticed. The staff carried the women below deck, smiling and laughing to passerby as though they were merely helping two guests who'd overindulged. Varka watched the entire ordeal from his lofty hiding place above the balustrades, working out how best to continue. The guests would obviously be easy to skirt, but the staff were attentive and disciplined. A direct approach with them would likely be unavoidable.

Slinking along the guide ropes and sails, Varka wove his way to the canvas roof of the main bar. Waiting for the bartender to take the next order, Varka fell like a melting shadow and landed right beside her. He pulled from his bandoleer a leather pouch tied off with wire. Inside the pouch was a poison Varka had purchased from the borders of the Dark Side. In its powdered form the substance was purest and potent, only the tiniest pinch needed for a heavy dose. However, there were a lot of guests and he wasn't sure if the alcohol would dilute it. Varka emptied the entire pouch throughout the bar's stock, concealed by his Wisdom and the distractions around him. The bartender had already poisoned three people by the time Varka retreated to his hiding spot.

He wanted to watch in order to make sure the poison did its job, but he had to keep moving. Varka scaled the masts once more and made his way to the Ecstasy's other watering holes. This part of the heist was tedious and would take hours, but it was necessary.

After corking the final cask, Varka nestled himself on a cross beam of the main mast. He dismissed his shadows and called his Wisdom to his hands instead. Fingertips glowing a dull jade, Varka rubbed the magic into his eyes and his ears, tickling him to the brink of insanity. The feeling lasted for only a few seconds however, and when Varka opened his eyes his enhanced senses assaulted him with stimuli. His vision zoomed like a hawk while his hearing amplified itself several times over. Dizzy and disoriented, he steadied himself against the main mast before chancing a glimpse at the decks below.

The crowds thinned to only a few stumbling stragglers. Varka couldn't believe how quickly the poison worked. He waited a bit longer, observing instead the roaming staff, who all wore looks of annoyed confusion. Varka could hear them all over the roaring spray of the ocean. With his eyes and ears he followed a servant carrying a broad tray crowded with drinks.

"What's up with this lot huh?" The servant slid the heavy tray down onto the bar with a grunt. "You couldn't clear a deck that fast even if it was on fire."

"You're not supposed to say 'fire' on the ship, moron," the bartender snapped, heaving a small cask up into a stained glass cabinet. She pulled a set of keys from her pocket and twirled them on her finger. "Saying 'fire' *gets* you fired."

"No one here to hear me say it, is there?" He waved his arm behind him to the empty deck. "Unless you'd like to turn me in."

She wiped her brow with a rag from her waist. "Bet you'd like that. Then I'd have to do your job too." She selected a key from her ring and started locking the cabinets.

"Whoa whoa whoa, not so fast then." The servant leaned close, casting a furtive glance about the deck. "Seeing as no one's here to see us, why don't we have a pull off that moonwine? Those lushes didn't drink much, they won't miss it."

A sly grin pulled at the corner of the bartender's mouth. "You really are trying to get fired."

Varka smiled to himself. Now there were two less to worry about. After waiting for a few of the more degenerate crew members to sneak their drinks from the poisoned stock, Varka descended from his hiding place and made for the helm. The ship was almost barren. Nearly all of its occupants were tucked in by his sleeping poison. It would have been easier to use a lethal poison, but that would have been taking more than the honest swindler's share.

Pulling his shadows close, Varka entered the helm, appearing as though a rude ocean breeze had blown the door open. A moment later, the captain and his two helmsmen nodded off as thin trails of sleeping poison crept unseen up their noses. Varka stowed the bodies in the nearest lifeboat. He had to dismiss his shadows momentarily to shift his Wisdom to lightening the hefty captain and his staff. After the helm, he worked his way through the crew next, starting from the higher ranking officers and ending his sweep with kitchen and laundry staff. A few required physical interaction, as they moved around too much or the wind carried the poison away, but it was easy enough to lure them to a shadowy corner. Varka was no fighter, and he refused to use the red magic on those who didn't deserve it. A proper application of stealth and the exploitation of complacency were far more effective for jobs such as this. After an hour the entire crew was sound asleep in their lifeboats, bobbing and dreaming in the calm waters of Galdebreah Bay. With the crew out of the way, Varka returned to the lower decks to jettison the passengers. The tedious work of poisoning the bars paid dividends, as he could devote his Wisdom to making the passengers light as pillows. He carried them out four at a time.

Varka was quite sure that he was the last person on the ship, but a cautious voice in the back of his mind suggested he make one more pass. Dismissing his shadows and sharpening his ears, he took a servant's passway to the lower decks. Before he reached the bottom he heard a distant drumming on his ears. A heartbeat thrummed softly and steadily just a few rooms away. It was far too slow to be a rodent, and as he crept closer he picked up traces of something tantalizingly fragrant. His search brought him to a cabin which Varka was positive he'd already checked, yet the throbbing heart called him in. As he pushed the door open, the tempting scent washed over him as he beheld the beautiful woman from the card game.

Varka pushed his way in, noting also a heavy scent of alcohol in the air. Miss Everbeam was sprawled face up. Only half her body was in the bed, as if she'd barely made it before the sleeping poison took her. Varka drew close, his eyes taking liberties they certainly would not have if she were awake. Time seemed to slow like cold honey.

An adventurous fire ignited from deep within a place into which Varka had never delved. Exploring her features was like exploring a treacherous jungle, marvelous yet deadly. Ribbons of auburn hair flowed in a wild mess of shiny curls and waves. Her brow was scrunched, hinting at some sad dream. Varka's gaze wandered farther down, taking in the lush petals of her lashes and perilous angles of her cheeks. Her lips looked as if they were capable of killing a man with the right word or granting his most intimate fantasy. It had been a long while since Varka had lain with a woman. So long that he couldn't even remember the town, let alone a name. This was a woman who deserved proper courting, but not now. Maybe another day. Perhaps another life. He only wished he could have one last look into her eyes.

Varka broke his gaze from the inviting folds of her breasts, which rose and fell with steady cadence. He had completely forgotten what he was here for, and he apparently forgot that he was supposed to be breathing. With a sharp intake of breath, Varka noticed a fist on his chest, the pommel of a dagger gripped within.

Varka raised a hand to hers, but as he did the dagger twisted, halting him. Judging by its location, he knew death was just a breath away. She had him now.

His gaze wandered cautiously from the wound, finding her pale blues. She did not look alarmed, nor angry. Her brow and lips were curled in a wry smile. Varka breathed a chuckle through the rising pain. At least he got one last look into those eyes.

The dagger twisted again, stealing his breath and stabbing lighting up his spine. He was suddenly very cold.

"Hyacinth," Varka whispered.

Her eyes narrowed. "What?"

"That's what you smell like." Varka smiled.

Her countenance softened, as if somehow disarmed, though her grip was as iron. Varka decided in that moment that he loved this woman, and he would die a man in love. If this was to be his execution, then he would have his final meal, whiskey and all. His hands came up once again, not to the wound, but to her face. He held her with his eyes just as she held him with the blade. With his precious seconds rushing out of him, Varka wove his fingers through the thick ropes of her auburn hair, pulling her lips into his. The last thing he remembered was the taste of fire and life on his tongue.

CHAPTER 4

A TEMPTING CONTRACT

Varka woke with a fuzzy throbbing in his head. His mouth was dry and his tongue felt like a slab of bark. He looked around, noting the familiarity of the room, though he couldn't quite place it. Mercifully, there was a pitcher of water on the nightstand. He reached for it, and as he did a bolt of paralyzing agony shot through his chest.

"Ah, yes. The dagger," Varka groaned as the memories came flooding back into his dull brain.

Shoving a pillow under his shoulder to support himself, he gripped the handle of the pitcher and spent the next minute carefully gulping it down. After quenching the fire in his throat, he took a moment to examine his injury. The wound had somehow healed while he slept. He peeled back the dressing and saw the skin whole and smooth. This was not nature's work, not unless he'd been asleep for weeks.

Varka rose to his feet, the stabbing pain in his chest setting the pace for his timid movements. Once his head stopped spinning he found that he had full use of his Wisdom, so he called it to his aid. He considered amplifying his senses or fashioning a weapon, but what was the point? If the blue-eyed woman wanted him dead then he would be. She certainly wouldn't have left him unrestrained and patched his wound. Varka tasked his Wisdom with lightening his body until he was no heavier than the clothes he wore. The pain in his chest lifted commensurately.

The cabin door was unlocked. The woman either had vacated the Ecstasy or she didn't consider him a threat. Judging by the smooth hum of the ship it was the latter. Varka bounded up the steps, eager to properly meet the woman who'd bested a master thief. As he cracked open the door a powerful gust of wind tore it from his grip, battering it against the wall. A cascade of blinding sunlight hit him full on. Varka squinted, adjusting his eyes with a quick spell. The Ecstasy's speed was even greater than the local tales lauded her for. They had already traveled to the light of Shaskein's star, a distance that would have taken any other ship a month.

Varka took one precipitous step at a time. Even after returning his body weight to normal, the wind constantly threatened to yank him across the deck. He considered casting another spell to find the woman, but there could only be one place for her at the moment.

Crawling his way up the highest stairs, Varka took a moment to nurse his spiking chest before shoving his way into the helm.

She stood next to the wheel, poring over a panel of lights and knobs with an air of uncertainty. She flashed him one of her pale blue eyes before returning to her work. She had relieved herself from the alluring party dress, wearing instead a sturdy cloth jacket and pants. Her hair fell in a waterfall of mahogany curls down her back. Panting, Varka fell into a helmsman's chair before the blackness could dominate any more of his vision.

"Was I right?" Varka asked.

"About what?" She didn't bother looking at him.

"About the hyacinth. Black-velvet hyacinth." Varka grinned as she shot him a nasty glare. She returned to the star charts and resumed her stony silence. "You don't seem the least bit surprised by my entering the helm. It's almost as if you were expecting me. How do you know I wasn't coming up here to take my revenge on you?"

"I didn't." She turned a dial on the corner of a star chart. In the center of the panel a sheet of lights shifted from white to red as the machine emitted an angry buzzing. She grunted and slammed the metal panel with her fist.

"How do you know I won't take my revenge on you now?" Varka turned his chair so he faced her straight on.

"You can't," she stated. Her confidence told him she truly believed it. "You're a Wisdom-user. You're no threat to me."

"So that's how you bested me?" Varka reached his hand over the controls, pushing a lever down. "I should have recognized another Wisdom-user."

"Don't touch that," she snapped, slapping his hand away and inching closer to him. "And no, I'm not a Wisdom-user."

"Then what manner of magic do you wield? There's no commoner alive that could have stopped me from taking the Ecstasy." Varka's fingers crawled closer to another lever.

"That's none of your concern. I said keep your hands off-" She lunged for him, one hand clamping firm on his wrist while a dagger wheeled around in the other. She was too late, however.

With a heavy thunk from beneath the console, a seam split in the middle of the floor, creating a neat circular opening the size of a dinner plate. From the hole rose a pedestal with a broad oval stone embedded in the top. The stone was polished as smooth as half-melted ice. A rose-colored light blushed from its cloudy depths.

She released her grip and sheathed the dagger behind her back. Wonder blossomed on her face as her eyes and her mouth popped wide. She seemed to float across the room, hands outstretched. "That's a Passion stone."

Varka watched from his chair, taking in the look of supreme desire on her face, wishing she would look at him like that. His head spun for an entirely different reason now.

She cupped her hands around the stone, running her fingers over the gold wire that embellished its surface in flowery swoops. The rosy light pulsed brighter at her touch.

"So that's what your magic is called." Varka joined her at the oval gem, sliding his fingertips over the frictionless surface.

"Yes." She pressed her cheek to the stone, closing her eyes as if embracing an old lover. "It is the magic of the heart."

"Was it your heart that stabbed me in the chest or stitched up the wound afterwards?" Varka fingered the hole in his shadow suit.

Her face sharpened as she measured him. "Necessity demanded I murder you." After inspecting him head to toe she turned with a whip of her hair, stalking back to the star chart. "I had a change of heart."

"Oh?" Varka limped after her. "And what had I done to earn the favor of a lady's heart?"

She kept her eyes on the charts. "Keep your venom behind your teeth, snake. It was only a turn of phrase. I kept you alive because you may be of use to me. You're obviously a master thief, which makes you a man of opportunity. I propose an opportunity to you now."

"You give me little choice. Let's have your offer." Varka sighed, returning to the chair. While he was still seriously injured, he was not entirely helpless. He could feel the red magic within him now, barking and thrashing for release. He didn't know much about this Passion, but he wouldn't put his money on this woman should he unleash his inner monster. He stilled the red magic for the sake of finding out why this woman intrigued him so, and the fact that he would likely destroy the Ecstasy.

"A wise man indeed." A grin pulled at her lips as she took on a seductive tone. Varka thought he felt something alluring and exotic fill the air between them. It could only be the woman's Passion. "Like yourself, I am a thief. I've never met a man I couldn't convince to give me whatever I desired. However, unlike yourself, I cannot wield Wisdom. While my Passion has yet to fail me, it does have its limitations. I propose that we work together. You and I, on the fastest ship on Aeneria. We could hit every trade port with impunity and be gone before the idiots figured out what we stole."

Varka was certain it was her Passion that soothed his doubts. He wanted nothing more than to please her, to touch her. Ever so quietly, he drew just a pinprick of the red magic. His nostrils and eyes flared as blood drummed in his ears. Before the fire could spread into action, Varka stifled the battle lust. The Passion crumbled to useless ashes within him. Clearing his mental canvas with a gust of Wisdom, he addressed the woman.

"I never work with a partner. One of those old tenants maintained by us master thieves. It's bad practice you see. Trusting another thief will land you with an empty purse, or a dagger in the heart." He pulled the hole in his shadow suit as wide as it would go, showing her the raw pink scar.

"I could always put the blade back," she mused playfully, now flipping her dagger in her hand.

It was now or never. Varka could call the red magic and be done with her. He would find a new Ecstasy and start over. What would stop her from killing him when he was no longer useful to her?

Unbidden, the red magic snuck loose from its bonds. It incinerated his rational thought and curiosity, replacing them with a supreme desire for violence. He stifled the magic once again, berating himself for his lack of vigilance. In the subsequent quiet, he felt something else within him. It was unlike anything he'd ever known. The thing was weak and brittle, though somehow unfazed by the force from the red magic. It was a budding plant, nestled deep within his sub-self. A black-velvet hyacinth of all things. Varka trickled a few drops of wonder into the tiny green shoot.

Returning from his daydream, he poured himself back into her pale blue eyes. "I will work with you."

"Beautiful." She clapped the stone and stepped close to Varka, placing a gleaming lavender finger to his wound. "You've earned yourself two days' worth of healing."

"How generous of you-oh," Varka's breath fluttered as the wound itched in a gratifying sort of way. When she lifted her finger his chest still pained him, but breathing was a little easier. "And what must I do for you to fix it properly?"

"That depends on if you prove yourself worthy of fixing." She winked and returned to the star chart.

"I see." Varka massaged his chest with tender fingers. "I should have mentioned, I have one stipulation for our contract."

She flashed him a derisive grin. "And what might that be? Keep in mind I control how fast that wound heals."

Varka ignored her. He winced as he shuffled to join her next to the star chart. Walking was only slightly less painful. He waited for her to look him in the eye before speaking. "I would know your name before we go any further. Not the one you use at card tables," he added.

She huffed, shaking her head as if he asked too much. Her hands and eyes returned to the star charts, which she appeared to still be struggling with. After a moment's silence she mumbled, "It's Vex."

Varka nodded slowly. Her hesitance told him she rarely shared this name with many people. "Would you care to know my name?"

"No," she said without looking up.

Varka sighed. It was obvious she had no idea how to work the star charts. The display was now entirely blank and a microphone had just descended from the gauges above.

Varka smiled and bowed as far as his injury would allow. "Well then Vex, if you'll excuse me I'm going to nurse this wound and put on something a bit more practical. Come find me when you have need of my assistance."

Chapter 5

A Name, Sweet One

Varka's wound was slow to heal, though over the passing week he swindled Vex into healing him in exchange for small favors. Most of these favors included proper lessons on the Ecstasy's systems, which required a measure of Wisdom to fully understand. Following a set of cables that ran along the promenade, Varka found a latch with a neat brass label that read *sheet cap*. After some fiddling with the latch, a clear canvas veil snapped over the upper decks, sealing it from the blustery wind. The trick earned him another three days' worth of healing. Each day Varka gifted her another of the Ecstasy's hints, and Vex gave him a trickle of Passion in return. Varka soon found himself doing extra favors, not for his injury, but to feel her Passion working in him. He yearned for the touch of her soul rubbing against his while she worked her magic on him. Though he didn't know why, he was still just as enamored by her as when she first shoved her blade between his ribs. Perhaps even more so.

"Get up here!" Vex's voice blared from a brass horn mounted atop the helm. "I need you to look at something."

Varka lay stretched out on a sun chair, engrossed in a book he'd found in the luggage of a jettisoned passenger. He had heard her of course, but he had a good reason for not answering. He flipped another page of his book.

"I know you can hear me!" she bellowed, her voice crackling over the horn. "Don't make me come all the way down there."

Varka flicked to the next page.

"I swear I'll stab you in the ass next if you don't move it!" Vex waited just another heartbeat before slamming the helm door shut and storming down the stairs. "Stupid, stupid man! I knew I should have killed him." She charged across the deck, now looming over Varka and casting him in her shadow. She yanked the book from his hands. "Look at me at least!"

Varka squinted, putting on a guise of confusion. "Were you talking to me this whole time?"

"Of course I was!" Vex hissed, hurling the book across the deck. "Who else could I be talking to? You were the one who tossed the rest of the passengers, idiot."

"Certainly, but that doesn't mean your badgering was directed at me. You could have been cursing the sun for all I know. There was no indication that you were talking to me directly. None whatsoever." Varka retrieved the book with a casual flick of Wisdom, the tome fluttering back into his open hand like a pet bird. "I do apologize for the confusion, I just wish there were some way we could avoid it. Perhaps some sort of title or moniker, unique to me so there'd be no mix ups…"

Vex bit down on her lips and pinched the bridge of her nose. "Fine. You win."

He gave her a mischievous smirk. "My dear Vex, I'll follow you anywhere, but I'm afraid I don't follow you on this. What did I win?"

Vex shook her head slightly as she sighed, "What is your name?"

Varka's mouth popped open: "Why that has to be the simplest, most beautiful solution to our quandary. I-"

"Give me your name," She crossed her arms, "And stop gloating, it's unattractive."

Varka rose to his feet, dipping into a low bow. "My name is Varka, and I am most humbly at your service."

"Whatever. Follow me." She stormed back towards the helm's stairs. Varka followed, tucking the book under his arm. "What are you reading anyway?"

"Oh this? It's a dossier on the Ecstasy. She's barely a cycle old, but the history here is remarkable." Varka took the steps two at a time while skimming through a few pages. "Did you know the Ecstasy is the sole surviving artifact from a battle on the Dark Side? Apparently the vessel had just departed on her maiden voyage when her port was sacked. The whole town was razed by marauders. Not a soul survived. The captain only got news of it when they stopped in another city."

"Lucky for the captain," Vex said in a hollow voice as she opened the door to the helm.

"Luck had nothing to do with it," Varka said, snapping the book shut and following her in. "The very captain who greeted us on the gangway was a war chief among the marauders. He and his band had boarded the Ecstasy before the proper crew. They have been working on the ship ever since. I suppose they grew tired of marauding and decided to give legitimate business a try."

"You read all this in that book?" Vex turned to him, genuinely curious.

Varka shook his head. "Absolutely not. This book is nothing more than carefully curated propaganda. No, I've been tracking the captain for nearly a cycle now. His secrets were scattered throughout a few of the larger towns I work in."

"Work? That's what you call it?" Vex let out a derisive chuckle. "The rest of us thieves just call it *stealing*."

Varka sat himself in the captain's chair. "Stealing is an oversimplification of the craft. Snatching a man's purse while he's looking the other way, that's stealing. Investigating and networking, reconnaissance and analysis, creating specific potions and spells for the job, all of this and more culminates into a single moment that can change a world."

"That does sound like work," Vex raised a contemplative eyebrow, "Though I suppose all that build-up makes for a greater reward in the end."

Varka leaned closer, taking in the scent of hyacinth. "I find the greatest reward in swindling other thieves. The captain was a master, albeit in his own savage way. I bested him."

"And *I* bested *you*." Vex's pale blue eyes softened as they flowed into him.

"That you did." Varka held her eyes for a moment, fighting the urge to lean closer. "What did you need help with?"

Vex blinked her black petal lashes. "It's the star charts. I think they might be broken."

"You mean *you* might have broken them?" Varka said with a smirk.

"Can you fix them or not?" She sighed, cocking her head.

Varka rose from his chair and sauntered over to the blank screen. A little red bulb in the corner blared furiously up at him. "I suppose I could take a look. How many days of healing would you rate this task?" he asked, tapping his sternum.

"Fix it and I promise I won't stab you again." She patted her dagger.

"What a deal." Varka rolled his eyes. "I hope your sense of mercy doesn't match your sense of humor- ouch!" Varka coughed, rubbing his ribs.

"I didn't say anything about punching," she jested, readying another strike. "Now do your Wisdom thing before I change my mind."

"Right away, good lady," Varka groaned. He considered the cluster of dials and buttons before him. Hiding his smile, he arbitrarily pushed every button on the panel, gaining nothing more than a warning buzz from the angry red light's speaker. He hid his laughter as Vex's eyes burned holes through his fingers. Only when he was certain she was about to reach for her dagger did he snap a black toggle three times. The screen flashed to white and the red light stopped its blinking. "Ah, there it is."

Vex let out a breath. "Finally. Your Wisdom works in the most odd ways."

He turned to her, admiring how the sunlight painted her face through her tangle of auburn hair. "That had nothing to do with Wisdom."

Her brows met. "Then what manner of magic was that?"

"The magic of reconnaissance," Varka said with a wink. "I spent a half hour in here under the guise of a curious traveller. The crew was most helpful after a few promises and some careful flattery. Charming others is closer to your form of magic, is it not?"

"That is one facet of Passion." Vex leaned into him for a better view of the panel, seemingly unaware of her bosom pressing into his arm. "What else did you learn from the crew?"

Varka swallowed. "Watch and learn, sweet one." He then showed her the correct sequence of dials and buttons. "This should bring up Shaskein's starscape."

The panel flashed black, then filled with a mess of twinkling stars and a compass. Varka waited for Vex's appraisal, but she'd wandered off to the back of the helm.

"There's another panel back here with that same layout. I wonder if it does the same thing." She stared hard at the panel. "I'm going to do it."

"Curiosity is the seed of discovery," Varka said, and nodded in encouragement. He took a step towards the center of the room, sharpening his ears with magic so he could hear if anything went awry.

In stark contrast to her initial fumblings, Vex worked the panel as fluently as if she'd been doing it all her life. With the final button pressed, heavy shutters snapped over all the windows, leaving the room aglow with dull lavender from the Passion stone. At first it appeared nothing else had occurred, but then little beads of light popped into existence in the domed ceiling of the helm. It was as if a drizzle of stars was raining down on them. Countless thousands of shimmering diodes hung in the air around them. Varka caressed his hand through them. The miniature stars bumped off his hand, zapping his skin before bobbing back to their rightful place.

Eyes lit with wonder, Vex swept across the helm and gave the wheel a gentle spin. Varka felt the ship lurch to the side, but the phantom starscape around them swirled in the opposite direction. The device was obviously calibrated for Shaskein's sky. This meant that they could use the stars to navigate even during the day.

Vex drew close. Varka inhaled slowly, savoring her fragrance. The Passion stone bathed half of her mischievous smile in lavender glow. Several urges welled up within Varka. It was all he could do to keep himself standing still.

She raised an eyebrow. "Are you ready for our first job?"

"I'll follow you anywhere, sweet one." Varka then took her hand. To his surprise she didn't object, though the look in her eyes told him she had nearly gone for her dagger. With an effort, he dismissed his desires and called upon his Wisdom. He traced a finger over her wrist as an emerald spark connected their skin. When he pulled away there was a wreath of crystalline hyacinth buds wrapped around her wrist. With another gentle nudge the petals changed from conjured emerald to black velvet. From within his sub-self, Varka felt his own budding plant take a few more drops, stretching and growing just a little more.

Vex cradled her wrist to her chest. "I…why would you do this?"

"I can remove it," Varka blurted, suddenly feeling foolish.

Vex twisted away. "No. I like it."

Varka gave her a weak smile, drawing her eye up. "Well then, you'd better not kill me or it will vanish. It needs a constant stream of Wisdom to keep it corporeal."

For the first time since they met, Vex really smiled at him. It was not one of her calculated acts of seduction, nor a derisive grin. It wasn't even physically attractive in Varka's eyes, more like the giddiness of a child. It was a genuine reaction to something wholesome, a fleeting glimpse into her soul. For the first time, Varka saw a glimmer of the real Vex. His love for her swelled just a little more.

CHAPTER 6

AMOSKEAG

After weeks of swift sailing, the Ecstasy had nearly drained all of its power from the Passion stone. Vex charged the stone daily, allowing them to make the long journey to their destination. Amoskeag was one of the largest trade ports on the planet. The city was home to the deepest pockets as well as the most fanatical zealots. There were several religious factions circulating about the city, each fighting for popularity among its denizens. As Amoskeag was as far as could be from Aeneria's Dark Side, the city had little to no dealings with magic. Where magic might provide logical answers, the city relied upon fables and ancient scrolls to discern life's greatest questions. One of the more popular subjects of contention was the meaning behind the changing starscapes and local planets. The factions believed the transient planets to be the avatars of their various deities, each fighting for control of the skies. However, a quick glimpse with Wisdom or even a strong telescope would show that Aeneria was the transient one, merely a visitor passing through realities.

Varka and Vex had spent the final day of their voyage altering the ship to appear as non-magical as possible. They stowed the decorations below deck as well as the portable heating towers, alcohol, potions, and string lights. It may not have appeared so to the untrained eye, but almost everything on the ship was powered in some way by the Passion stone.

"Why are we stripping the entire ship again?" Vex grunted, following Varka below deck with an armful of wooden music boxes.

Varka kicked a cabin door open with a gust of Wisdom, dumping his load onto the bed. "Amoskeag abhors all things from the Dark Side. As hostile as the zealots are towards each other, they all treat anything from the Dark Side like a plague. They take great care to maintain their cloak of ignorance. Spend a good portion of the taxpayers' money on it too. If their citizens knew the truth of the world, then the factions would lose their power to a government run by logic. They'll defend that power with swift executions of any infidel that asks too many questions."

Vex threw her music boxes on the bed next to Varka's. "I knew Amoskeag were a bunch of idiots, but I never thought them dangerous. Looks like I picked the right assistant for this job." Her face suddenly lit up and she bolted back upstairs.

"Something wrong?" Varka called, running after her. The wound in his chest stung with every step.

Her voice echoed down the stairwell. "There *will* be if the port authorities see a ship floating ten feet above the water."

Once the Ecstasy was nestled safely in the waves, they took a much slower pace into the Amoskeag docks. As they drew near, Varka took control of the wheel, bringing them away from the main piers. Vex punched him in the arm.

"I was managing just fine. Is your masculinity in peril, my lord? Afraid someone might see a woman bringing you into port?" She jabbed a finger towards the docks. "You're going the wrong way."

"I'm bringing us to a pier owned by one of the local guilds." Varka shot her a warning glare. "I have credit with them, and most importantly they won't inspect our vessel."

"How do we know they can be trusted?" Vex demanded.

"They can't." Varka squinted at the shore, ignoring her noises of protest. "Which is why we're going to invite them to raid the cabins."

Vex took a step back, looking him up and down as though she'd never seen him properly. "Varka my dear, it is very important that you explain to me why we're letting a gang of thieves raid the Ecstasy."

"You may not believe it, but the guilds are the true sovereignty of any large city." Varka gave the wheel a quarter turn. "They are the blood that flows through the city's veins, the dreams that guide the masses. The guild has eyes and ears everywhere and they rarely miss a trick. Any thief who fancies himself a bold rogue, say skimping on guild dues or taking an unsanctioned job, will find himself under their heel of judgment before long."

34

"This guild sounds no worse than any other tax-mongering oligarchy. What do we get in return for giving them a cut of our labors?" She cracked open a window, filling the helm with fresh, briny air. A fat sea bird flew alongside the Ecstasy, searching for a good place to land.

"It's not as bad as it sounds, or as costly," he said, softening his voice. "The guild collects its dues like taxes; however, they have no need for things like infrastructure or government programs. Their budget is used to keep order among the chaos so that a town is not over-hunted. Guild-sanctioned jobs keep things sustainable and discreet. Membership provides certain benefits, such as access to their bribery networks, their lists of vulnerable marks, and black market supplies from the Dark Side. You make a name for yourself among the guild and the perks only get better. It's all very lucrative actually." Varka gave her a sideways grin. "I could put in a good word for you."

Vex huffed. "I work better alone. You're the only exception I've made in my entire career and I'm still not sure." She frowned, eyes searching the floor. "Are they going to take everything from the cabins? The luggage alone has to be worth as much as the ship. We could slip right into the town docks. I'm confident my Passion would keep anyone from asking too many questions."

"I'm sure you'd have the port authorities charmed around your little finger, but not the guild. They already know we're here."

"How could you possibly know that?" Vex shot him a suspicious glare. "Unless you tipped them off with your Wisdom."

"Hardly." Varka shook his head. "I'm not that adept with the magic. The guild has agents everywhere. Stealing a magical luxury-vessel isn't going to happen without notice, or their approval. I paid their Galdebrean chapter in advance to sanction a mark on the Ecstasy. Offering up the contents of the cabins will cover whatever job you have planned for us. And besides, dropping some weight will make the Ecstasy all the swifter."

Vex gave him an appraising smile as she caressed the petals of her bracelet. "I knew of the guild, but I had no idea its influence was so vast. I'm glad I did not kill you."

Varka locked his eyes forward as a wave of Passion rushed into him. His toes twitched as the tingling warmth wandered over every inch of him. He swallowed, suddenly very hot. "I would have died a happy man."

He chanced a glimpse at her. Her eyes were on his chest, staring at the wound beneath the shirt. She bit her lip, looking as though she wanted to say something. Varka reached for her hand, but her face broke into her childlike smile as her hands darted for the controls. The Ecstasy slowed as the wheel locked itself immobile in Varka's hands.

She grabbed him by the hem of the shirt, beckoning him along: "Come!"

Varka laughed, bouncing on his toes to keep from falling. "Where to, fine lady?"

"To raid the cabins before your friends empty them." She threw open the door and pulled him down the stairs. "We'll have to change our clothes before we arrive anyway. You're a bit underdressed for our party."

"What party?" Varka demanded, doing his best not to trip over her feet as she dragged him along. "You still haven't told me about the job by the way."

"Oh, I'm sorry." She whisked him through the promenade, strumming her fingers along the ribbed base of a fountain. "I thought you were a master thief. I didn't think you needed a briefing from a lowly swindler such as myself."

Varka opened the promenade door with a flick of Wisdom. "Last I checked this master thief was bested and spared by a *lovely* swindler. There's nothing lowly about you, my dear."

"And don't you forget it!" Vex's laughter echoed down the halls of the lower deck. Still running, she released his hand and undid the buttons of her shirt before throwing the garment in his face.

Varka chased after her, stripping himself down while dodging the rest of her clothes. With the Ecstasy now chopping as slowly as a common ship it would take all night to reach the guild docks. Vex ran far ahead, her naked leg disappearing through the door of a cabin they had yet to sleep in. Varka was certainly in no rush to end their little cruise.

Chapter 7

The Greater the Risk…

The Ecstasy bobbed into the guild docks, nestling into an unobtrusive alcove just out of sight from foot traffic. Sporting a very uncomfortable set of gold and white ceremonial robes, Varka strode down the gangway with Vex on his arm. Vex wore a fluffy powder-blue dress and a veil that hid her eyes. The dock hands did a poor job of hiding the hunger on their faces. Their eyes burned down the length of the Ecstasy and the two hapless nobles that had wandered into the guild's open arms. A dozen figures slinked out from behind barrels and shacks, each heading their way with their hands behind their backs. Vex's hands tightened on Varka's arm. Before the dock lead could say a word, Varka recited the poem that was the guild's password.

The dock lead's face went from greedy grin to washed surprise as he waved his comrades back to their shadows. Varka squared up with the guild representative, leaving clear instructions as to what cargo would be offered as tribute. Varka's casual banter with the other guild members seemed to put Vex at ease. The dock workers took no notice of them as they walked the length of the pier. Vex gasped her surprise to see a carriage waiting for them at the base of the dock. A hulking engine flexed out the back side and its fat tires looked better suited for off-road use.

"Just another guild perk." Varka bowed, opening the door for her.

"I loathe these machines. So loud and bumpy." Vex leaned around, gazing at the empty driver's seat. "Is this carriage driven by wishes and dreams?"

"Of a sort. Hop in." Varka leaped into the plush seat ahead of her. "Trust me."

Vex shook her head and pulled herself in. Varka folded the middle seat down, showing her a dim oval stone. Her eyes lit. "Another Passion Stone?"

"Wisdom," Varka said, clapping his palm to the smooth surface. The stone flashed a brilliant green as an outline of a man materialized in the driver's seat. His face was featureless and cloaked in shadow, while white gloved hands gripped the wheel. The carriage lurched forward silent and smooth without a bump or sound. Varka indulged in Vex's astonishment. "The guild is one of the few places you'll find magic on the Light Side."

"I'm liking this guild more and more I think," she admitted, looking back to the Ecstasy, which was already being stripped of its tributary cargo. "After this job you will have to show me a few of your tricks with Wisdom."

"Only if you show me a trick or two with Passion," Varka replied, gesturing towards the phantom driver. "I know you're playing this job close to the chest, but you might want to tell him where we're going. And while you're at it I wouldn't mind knowing what we're doing."

"Oh fine." Vex pulled out a mirror and checked her hair, tucking a wandering strand back behind her ear. "Driver, take us to the Stratus Temple." The driver gave a mechanical nod, though the rest of him was still as a rock's shadow. His arms remained stationary while the wheel turned under his gloves.

"The Stratus Temple!" Varka hissed, turning in his seat to face her. "That place is under guild protection. We'd never get a sanctioned job at the temple. Even asking would be grounds for execution. Without guild approval it would take weeks of reconnaissance and bribing just to get through the front door. I think it's time you tell me your plan, and don't leave anything out. The slightest mistake could cost us our lives."

"Oh Varka, enough with your rules," she sighed, placing a hand on his knee. "You cling to them like a safety rope. Don't you ever want to try something new?"

Varka's cheeks flushed. "My rules have made me rich, and more importantly they've kept my neck out of the gallows."

"So you are afraid of risk then?" Vex asked, leaning closer.

Varka drew back. "That's not what I said."

"Then why do you do it? Why bother going through all that trouble for the sake of stealing? Surely with your cleverness and magic you could find a legitimate way to get yourself rich." Her voice softened: "Why are you still here?"

Varka did not answer. He looked out the window, watching Shaskein's low sun pop in between the passing buildings. A thought fell heavy over his mind like a lead coat. He realized Vex had just voiced a question that he'd been ignoring all along. Why *was* he still here? Everything he knew about Vex had gone against his better judgment. She was reckless and wild, and though she didn't kill him she certainly showed that she was willing to do so. Nothing about her style of work suited his own. Varka worked alone for a reason.

He returned his gaze to her, diving into her pale blues. Her face had a forced calm to it, as though she expected him to jump out of the carriage and leave her forever. She took her hand from his knee and hugged her belly. Her fingers clutched at the black velvet bracelet.

Vex's chest rose and fell as her eyebrows met in a sharp bump. "Without risk the job is just a job. The same could be said for life. You can calculate every step along the way and make sure you never get burned, or you can be the flame and dance through the winds of consequence. I burn, Varka, but I burn alone. I want you to burn with me."

A fathomless longing rushed up from places Varka had been raised to suppress. He stilled his mind, but his heart raced ahead, filling him with something that yearned to be acknowledged. He had grown accustomed to Vex's Passion meddling with his mind, and he was quite sure this was not her doing. He scanned the interior of the carriage as he searched within himself for the source of the feeling. He finally recognized it when he landed on her eyes once more. From deep within, he felt the tiny hyacinth crying out to him, begging for nourishment. Varka knew this was the point of no return. He could walk away now, before the plant's little roots took purchase on his soul. Or, he could feed it.

Pulling both of her hands into his, Varka let out a long breath. His life as he knew it was over. He poured everything he was into the little plant, blooming its flowers and stretching its roots. He gave her fingers a gentle squeeze. "I'll follow you anywhere, sweet one."

Vex relaxed and gave him her warm, childlike smile. "I knew you'd come around."

Chapter 8

Among the Clouds

The carriage slowed to a halt outside the single largest staircase Varka had ever seen. He'd heard tell of its grandeur, but his jobs in Amoskeag had never brought him within a mile of the Stratus Temple. He hopped out onto a polished marble walkway, holding his arm out for Vex. She brushed past him, whispering under her veil.

"I appreciate the chivalry, but we must play our parts now. You're wearing the ceremonial robes of an ulrich." She rushed ahead, making Varka jog to catch up.

Varka cast a wary look around him. He muttered under his breath, moving his lips as little as possible. "Are those the silent priests that have their tongues and … other things removed?"

"And they each serve a Cardinal, which is my part. Now stop talking." Vex gave a nod and quick bow to a regal priest in shiny mahogany robes.

Varka stowed his annoyance. Not only was he delving into the unknown with the most whimsical thief he'd ever encountered, he had do it with a bound tongue as well. As if she could hear his thoughts, Vex's gait slowed as she flashed him a smirk from under her veil. Varka dismissed his reservations and shifted his focus to the moment. This must have been part of the thrill Vex talked about. Varka thought it felt more like a cold knot of worms bouncing around his belly.

Hitching up her dress, Vex led him to a wooden shuttle-cart set into rails on the side of the stairs. A thick wire shot up the tracks, ending at the temple door. Varka thought it funny that not a single person took the stairs up or down. It was as if the towering steps were simply there as a barrier to dissuade the interest of common-folk.

At first glance, Varka thought a child was holding the shuttle door, ushering them onto the cart. Closer inspection revealed the child to be one of the little people. Varka felt bad for them. As if their knee-high stature and slavery weren't enough, the church had dubbed their race Underkin, solidifying their very name in the lowest caste.

The Underkin waited for a few more people to board before cranking a lever with both her hands. Like all Underkin her face appeared aged with heavy crinkles, though Varka could tell by the innocence in her eyes that she was quite young. He tried offering the girl a smile, but she kept her eyes locked below his knees.

A distant cranking shook down the thick wire, vibrating up Varka's legs as the cart ascended. The Stratus Temple looked more like a giant trophy than a place of worship. The stairs alone were taller than the surrounding buildings. Shaskein's golden sun lit one of the temple walls, displaying a host of carved deities that ran up its exterior. Each marble figure was locked in some epic pose of triumph or else casting haughty sneers down at the town below. The low sun stretched the temple's shadow for miles.

After a lengthy ride the shuttle clunked to a halt atop the stairs. The heavy wire that carried them up ended in a massive spool taller than Varka. As they stepped out onto the landing a chorus of panting and grunting drew Varka's attention. From within the spool, dozens of Underkin hung by leather straps. Tiny arms sagged, tired and spent as their little chests heaved for air. Varka felt suddenly sick. Before he stepped off, he coaxed his Wisdom into the cart, cutting its weight in half. The spell would only last an hour or so, but it was all he could afford to use facing an unknown heist. He wished there were more he could do. He looked to Vex, but the skirt of her dress was already disappearing through the main doors.

As he trotted to catch up, a pair of burly doormen stopped Varka in his tracks. Thick arms barred the way while swords scraped from their scabbards. Varka clapped his lips shut, nearly forgetting that he wasn't supposed to speak.

"Oh he's mine," Vex called from the atrium. She lifted her veil and flashed a mischievous smile to the doormen, who suddenly seemed to forget where they were. Varka recognized a warm wave of Passion wash over the doorway. "Come now ulrich, stop your dithering and keep up."

Varka pushed his way past the dumbstruck men. He adjusted his collar, which had started making his neck itch. Vex snapped her fingers and pointed to the floor directly behind her, indicating that he should follow closely. He rolled his eyes and took his position.

The entrance hall was lined with paintings resembling the deities on the temple's exterior. Gas torches flickered down the hall, which appeared to end in a room bathed in broad daylight. Vex slowed as the way became clogged with dignitaries moving in and out. By the various colors of their ceremonial attire it appeared that priests and Cardinals of every sect were gathered within. The parties exiting the temple rambled in loud, slurry voices and bumped along the walls. Varka didn't need to sharpen his senses with magic to pick up the scent of alcohol, or see the stains of shrikeshard dust in their eyes. Amoskeag's religious factions may disagree on legislature and history, but it seemed they found a commonality in mirth within the Stratus Temple. Varka pressed closer to Vex, keeping his Wisdom coiled and ready.

A chorus of chatter and orchestral music greeted them as they entered the great hall. Even if Varka were allowed to speak, he wouldn't be able to hear Vex over the din of hundreds. The temple looked nothing like any religious house Varka had ever encountered. It was as if whoever curated the great hall wanted to use every inch of the place to showcase its affluence. Walls of flowering plants swayed in the currents of passersby, some of which Varka recognized from the Dark Side. After probing the air with Wisdom, he found the support columns were not simply veneered, but solid gold all the way through. Everywhere he looked there were Underkin rushing in between legs, picking up dropped food or rushing fresh drinks to expectant hands. Varka knew the Stratus Temple was run by crooked priests, but this was beyond excessive. They took far more than the honest swindler's share. Vex's job seemed much more interesting to him now. Hopefully the guild didn't have eyes within the temple walls tonight.

Varka had been so busy inspecting the opulence around him that he lost Vex. He could have sworn she was nearby. He could hear, feel and smell her, like she was right next to him, but her powder blue dress was nowhere to be found.

"You're doing a horrible job at playing my ulrich," Vex's voice rang in his mind.

Varka jumped, resisting the urge to check under a nearby table. Had he imagined her saying that?

"No, you're not losing your mind." Her laughter fluttered in between his thoughts. Her voice was even loud and clear. *"But you are losing your Cardinal. Come find me by the fountain."*

Unsure of how to respond, Varka imagined his own voice shouting within his skull, *"Vex?"*

"Of course it's me," she snapped. *"Relax your face, you look like you're in need of a bathroom."*

Varka felt the wrinkles loosen on his forehead. *"How is this possible? This is a most peculiar thing."*

"It's just Passion. Frankly I'm surprised you were capable of completing the link on your end. You never said you could use other magic besides Wisdom." Her voice lingered after she spoke, like words written in the sand between waves.

Varka almost said that he couldn't use other magics, but that wasn't true. Even now he could feel the red magic burning at a low simmer. He stilled his mind, dumping the errant thought. Had she heard that as well?

Vex's laughter hummed like a song. *"Just come find me. I may have overdone my charming of these men and I could use an ulrich's presence. Hurry now, I'm by the fountain."*

Varka huffed. He trudged off towards the nearest fountain, only to find that there were at least a dozen scattered throughout the great hall. To his disgust, each was covered with several Underkin, all working tirelessly. They passed buckets in a chain, laboring to bring water back up to the top of the fountain in order to keep it flowing. Varka wove through the throngs of nobles and religious officials, now looking at the environment with a schemer's eye. If he were about to earn a lifelong ban from the guild, then he might as well do some damage to Stratus Temple on his way out.

Just when he thought he'd never find Vex, a fuzzy instinct brought him in a clearer direction. It was a guess, but the farther he walked the more lucid the urge became.

"Find me," Vex whispered into him. He knew he was going the right way.

Stepping around a crackling granite fireplace, Varka found her surrounded by several important-looking men. A few wore robes identifying them as high-ranking priests. Vex was clearly the center of their attentions; however, her smile grew more forced by the second. The men pulled her this way and that, trying to bring her close or else guide her away with a firm hand. Varka could feel strings of panic plucking through their link.

The red magic swelled, eager to defend her. His fingers twitched and hardened before he stifled the violent urges. No one needed to die tonight. He snatched a serving platter from a passing Underkin, swiftly nudging his way to Vex's side. Conversation halted in deathly quiet as he moved in between Vex and the priests. Brutality flashed and faded from their faces once they saw the drinks Varka offered. Greedy hands wiped the platter clean.

"Oh there you are!" Vex gushed, inching closer to him. "I thought you'd gotten yourself lost. Gentlemen, this is my ulrich. Ulrich, be a good boy and say hello to these fine men… *just shake their hands and keep quiet."*

The men looked at Varka as if he were a feral rodent begging for a heavy boot. Chests puffed and knuckles cracked. Most drew back, though one priest in purple robes locked his jaw and presented a massive hand. Varka gave the man a polite nod and reached out to shake it, but not before hardening the flesh of his hand with Wisdom.

"I would have expected such a fine Cardinal to have a more impressive ulrich," the man scoffed, grasping Varka's hand in a crushing grip. The man's fingers flexed and popped as he tried to crush Varka's, which were now harder than tempered steel.

Varka's grin broadened as the man strained. Finally, the priest released and Varka brought his hand to the others, giving them each an iron shake.

"My ulrich has plenty of ways to defend my honor." Vex patted Varka on the shoulder. "Look at him, so strong and quiet. If I only asked it of him he'd run to the horizon and back, or kill everyone in this hall and fill the fountains with their blood."

Varka stiffened as he handed the serving dish off to a passing Underkin. He wished he were watching the exchange from a dark shadow in the rafters. The spotlight was no place for a thief.

"I dunno, Cardinal, I still say this one's a bit soft for the job." The big priest sneered as he massaged his hand. Varka couldn't help but notice that he was the largest person in the hall. "An ulrich of his stature might be better off tending to the gardens or cleaning the gutters." His purple robes bounced up and down with his chuckling as he leaned close. His breath reeked of wine and onions. His eyes raked over Vex's gown, lingering over her chest. "You need a man of substance to satisfy your needs. Especially the needs of that tight little body of yours. What use is a castrated mute for a woman of your caliber?"

His sneer stretched to his ears as he looked back to his fellows. Emboldened by his confidence, the others roared with laughter as their drunken shuffling brought them closer. Varka felt the red magic flash up again, hot and starved. Their throats were wide open, begging his fingers to close around them.

"Strike the big one. Now," Vex demanded through their link. Her face remained calm as ever.

Varka called his Wisdom to the moment. The green magic slowed things for him, showing the simplest path through the puzzle. Lashing out, Varka swept his heavy iron fist across the inside of the larger man's knee. Alarm had barely registered in the man's eyes before pain took over, filling them with unruly tears. Silence fell over the surrounding crowds as the oaf crumpled to the floor.

As though nothing had happened, Varka snatched a husk of dark fruit from a startled Underkin, offering it to Vex. The other priests circled about their fallen comrade, hoisting him to his feet while keeping Varka in plain view.

"Come ulrich, I want to pay tribute at our altar," Vex called to him, setting off at a brisk pace.

"Wait, Cardinal! I didn't get your name!" A priest shot out from under the arm of the purple-robed priest.

"Please, don't leave yet!" said another, abandoning his injured friend. "When will I see you again?"

Varka stopped and turned on his heel, glaring at the advancing men as he prepared a spell to trip them both. They faltered and deflated before turning heel.

"That will do," Vex loosed a cooling breath into him. *"Don't trail too far behind. I can't look my part without you nearby."*

Varka suppressed a pang of annoyance as he darted after her. *"You know, it's typically better practice to not cause a scene while on the job. All eyes are upon us now."*

"This isn't my first job," Vex replied. Her tone was much less musical now. *"I did what was necessary."*

"Flirting those men into a frenzy was necessary?" Varka asked. *"They'll be after my blood before the end of the night. We'll have to find alternate means of egress now."*

To Varka's surprise, he sensed amusement trickling through the link. A smug grin snuck out from under Vex's veil as she led him to the back of the hall.

"May I be so bold as to educate the master thief, or are you beyond learning?" She hitched up her skirt and tiptoed her way down another flight of stairs. The din of the main hall died out as they descended.

Varka took a calming breath, centering himself. *"A master thief is never done learning, sweet one."*

Vex prodded him, tickling him with thought: *"How very wise of you, Wisdom-bearer. Your swift action against the large one is the proper response for an ulrich and will make others think twice before pestering me. I may have been a tad too heavy with the Passion, but I'm confident those men will start fighting over me at any moment, which will draw attention while we work. Also, charming those men yielded all sorts of useful information, to include the location of our target."*

"Now you're singing my tune." Varka sidled closer, indulging in her scent of hyacinth. The stairs brought them down to a tight hall with low ceilings. Candles of every color danced up rows of ebony support columns, making the hall look as though it had been painted by Oberon itself. *"I don't suppose you'd care to share what our target might be?"*

"I'll leave that little surprise till the end. Judging by your opinion of the Underkin's slavery, I think you'll appreciate what we're doing here." She slinked ahead of him. The inviting curves of her body were bathed in warm hues from the candles. There was little foot traffic in the hall, but her seductive gait drew sidelong glances from men and women alike. While her charming Passion wasn't directly aimed at Varka, he could feel it permeating the very air and strumming through their Passion-link. He admired her all the more for it. With magic like that she didn't need skill sets in reconnaissance and stealth. Not when her victims were enthralled by her very presence.

The foot traffic thinned as the candles dimmed. The hall led them to a shiny brass door guarded by two men in full ceremonial armor. Each man leaned on a tall rifle with leafy blades affixed to the end of its barrel.

Vex halted in front of the guards. She crossed her arms and huffed impatiently. "Are you paid to stand there and look tough or are you going to open the damned door?"

Varka stepped beside her, trying to look as large as possible while measuring the guards. His iron fist would be of little use against their heavy plate armor and he couldn't begin to guess how to disable their rifles. Hopefully Vex could talk her way through.

With eyes straight ahead, one of the guards slammed the butt of his rifle to the marble floor. "No one enters the Stratus Altars without credentials. Present your talisman to advance."

Varka was quite sure neither of them had credentials of any sort. The guards stiffened in the thick silence as their leather gloves creaked over their weapons.

Her warning streamed through their link, *"Don't do a thing."*

Vex sauntered close to the guards, running her fingers up the length of their rifles. A fiery tingle spread over Varka, as though someone had dumped a bucket of red-hot needles down his back. His vision blurred, and he recognized all too late that he had succumbed to the dose of Passion. Try as he might, he swayed on the spot, helpless as her charm commandeered his thoughts. All of Varka's concerns and goals faded below him, replaced by a single-minded desire to please her.

"I'm in such a hurry," Vex moaned. She slapped a hand on the brass doors, dragging a fingernail down the seam. "If I don't pay tribute at my altar before the close of day I'll lose favor with the church. Let us through, please. It would mean the world to me."

Varka's cheeks flushed. He ran through every spell he knew, desperate to find a way to break the door open before the guards, but oddly enough he couldn't recall a single spell. The air shimmered before him as both guards took on dreamy expressions.

"Stay with me now, Varka." Vex's mental voice was rough and loud, breaking Varka from his fantasies.

"Of course, Cardinal. Come on through." The guard on the left rushed at the door. His fingers scrabbled desperately over the handle, as though he couldn't get it open fast enough. The other guard merely admired Vex with his mouth agape. With a heavy clunk that shook the floor, the door swung open.

"Thank you boys. Come ulrich." Vex winked and grinned to Varka. She turned back to the guards once Varka was through. "Go ahead and shut the door. If you don't mention to anyone that you saw me then I might have a treat for the two of you when I return."

The guard who was still capable of speech gave her an eager nod and a salute. "By my honor."

The door shut with a solid thunk, closing them in a wide circular room. Surrounding the chamber were twenty-one shrines, each bedecked with candles and little statues. Vex donned a more relaxed gait as she rounded a pillar to the center, only to halt with a sharp breath.

Varka felt a pang of terror through their link. He peered around the pillar, stepping in front of Vex. Standing on the center dais was a woman who looked as if she didn't belong within a league of the temple. She was stick thin and very tall. Her body was wrapped tight in leather armor of a ruddy merlot color, giving her the appearance of having just emerged from a pool of old blood. Her hair was so fine and fair that it looked like a white cloud. It draped down to her narrow waist, billowing in currents unseen. Her face was almost featureless, encased in egg-white skin that stretched back into a high forehead. Varka had seen this woman before. His brief encounters with her in the guild halls told him that he never wanted to be the one to draw her attention. She may have been with the guild, but she was no thief. She was an assassin.

"Whatever you do, don't use any of your magic against this woman," Varka gripped their mental link, saturating it with the significance of the moment.

"Who is she?" Vex asked.

"Someone we don't want to annoy." He pushed Vex back a step.

The pale woman swept down the dais, her flat-black eyes locked right into Varka's. She was taller than he remembered, taking the steps two at a time. Bundles of silver wire bounced off her hips, each fastened to lengthy spikes strapped to her thighs. Fighting his instincts to simply bolt, Varka stood his ground and puffed his chest as a good ulrich would. He was reasonably sure she didn't recognize him. If she'd already marked him as a rogue-thief then he would have been dead long before he ever saw her.

The woman stopped a few paces from Varka. "Good evening, Cardinal." Her voice was rich and masculine. Varka had never heard her speak before, but now he wasn't sure if she was a woman at all. "May I approach? I wouldn't want to offend your ulrich."

"Of course," Vex's voice was steady, though her Passion link dwindled to a twitchy strand. Varka stepped aside. "But I'm afraid I don't have much time to dally. A Cardinal's callings rarely allow for idle chatter."

The woman inclined her head and smiled. Her grin was only made apparent by the appearance of greyish teeth. It looked as if she had no lips at all, that her paper-white cheeks simply fell into a hole above her chin. "I'll be concise then. I represent an organization that has a heavy interest in the welfare of the Stratus Temple. I ensure that our interests remain above risk, which is what brings me here tonight. We believe that there are individuals within the temple that do not belong here. These people intend to bring harm to the temple, perhaps even take something from it. Do you have knowledge of anyone who might fit that description?"

Vex's eyes sharpened as she took on a professional tone: "You must be new to your position. Around here it's generally not advisable to assume a Cardinal would be privy to the actions of degenerates. One might think you were accusing the church of something unsavory. If I weren't in such a rush I'd report you, as there's no good reason for odd creatures like you to skulk about the temple's inner sanctum. But fortunately for you I must take my leave. I suggest you do the same." Vex made a hard right and stormed off towards a shrine. Varka followed close behind.

"That's the wrong shrine, Cardinal," the woman's booming voice echoed across the chamber. "Your dress indicates that you serve Dunhaven. Dunhaven's shrine is over there."

Vex stiffened, doing a poor job of making it seem she was only admiring the nearby shrine before continuing to the next. Varka trailed behind, Wisdom glowing unseen inside his clenched fists. After passing a few more shrines he chanced a quick glance over his shoulder. The pale woman was still there, but her eyes were not on Vex. They were drilling into Varka.

When Vex came to Dunhaven's shrine the woman's leathers could be heard creaking softly towards the door, though her footsteps made no sound whatsoever. The door groaned wide as the woman's voice boomed across the chamber, "Stay pure, Cardinal."

Varka watched her leave through the reflection of a mirror. The doors thunked shut once more.

A minute passed and neither of them spoke. Varka strummed their link, letting Vex know it was safe.

She didn't move, however, speaking instead through the link, *"Is she really gone?"*

He angled his ears from side to side. *"I've sharpened my ears as much as I can with Wisdom. I can hear the heartbeats of the guards outside the door, but no one else."*

Vex exhaled, whipping around with a mixture of worry and anger on her face. "What in Oberon's light was that thing?"

CHAPTER 9

THE COLD CROW

"She has no name," Varka whispered, peering into every shadow. "Around the guild she is known as a Cold Crow."

"That thing is with your guild?" Vex said, giving him a look of sudden mistrust.

"The Cold Crows are assassins, separate from the guild. They are the enforcers. The ones who make sure we all toe the line." Varka shivered, feeling as though something wet and unsavory had somehow clung to his skin. "I've never heard one talk before, let alone drawn one's attention."

"Was it a woman?" Vex asked, hugging herself.

"It appeared so," Varka replied.

"There was something wrong about her, like she didn't belong here." Vex paled, looking close to vomiting. "She didn't feel Aenerian."

"I told you not to use your Passion on her!" Varka hissed, checking the door. "We already stick out like a couple of beggars in here. For all we know she'll come back and kill you out of curiosity."

Vex glared at him. "I didn't touch her. I even pulled back from our link as much as I could. Being adept with Passion attunes my senses to certain anomalies. That Crow-thing left a taint in my heart. And my skin feels like I've been doused with cold oil."

Varka rubbed the skin on the back of his neck. It was covered in chilled sweat. "I'm sorry. I felt it too."

She approached him and in one fluid motion placed a hand on his cheek. Varka felt their link thrum and swell as a rush of warmth and wholesomeness crashed into him, washing away all traces of the Cold Crow. On a whim, he pushed himself back through the link, reciprocating her empathy. To his delight, he felt a lessening of her dread.

"I'm very glad I didn't kill you," Vex said with a smirk, slapping his cheek. She turned towards the door, beckoning him along with her little finger. "You're a rare soul, Varka. Now let us be off. We'll have to settle for a less ambitious debut job."

A reckless urge taking him, Varka called his Wisdom. He reached out with invisible hands, wrapping them around Vex's waist and pulling gently. She let out a startled cry as she hovered a few inches off the ground, alighting on the dais in front of Varka. His mischievous grin wiped the uncertainty from her face.

"Giving up already?" Varka lowered his glowing jade hands. "It's bad luck to abandon your first job."

"Are you stupid?" Vex jabbed, adjusting the folds of her dress. "We were made. That Crow-thing probably knew what we were long before we ever stepped into the great hall. You said it yourself, the guild doesn't tolerate rogue thieves. I was all for the risk when there was a chance we'd go unnoticed, but there's no way now. We'll save this one for a rainy day, or when we the guild has a change of heart. Unless… you think you're a match for that thing?" She posed the question to him without a trace of sarcasm.

Varka chuckled softly. "Certainly not."

"Then why take the risk?" She sighed.

"I was exiled from my home because I didn't fit into the social machine that those before me had built. I was raised to believe that a flavorless life of logic and rules was the only clear path. I've come to realize that my life in the guild is just as narrow and limited. I yearn for change, just as I did then. As a boy I knew there were other paths I could take. Though these paths were wild and uncharted, I gave myself to them and felt my very soul on fire. It cost me everything, but I learned a great deal about myself. I burned. I feel it within me again. I burn for the thrill of this very moment. I burn for risk, and for the sweet promise of a swindler's victory." Varka took a deep breath, drinking in her fragrance as he cupped her face in his hands. "I burn for *you*, Vex."

He expected her to resist, but she came to him. Her arms wrapped over his shoulders as she brought her mouth to his. Hot lust poured through their link and over their tongues. Varka entwined one hand through her mess of auburn hair while grasping the small of her back with the other. He gripped her tight, feeling her moan vibrate through his teeth.

She pulled away first, wet lips pulling into her genuine smile. "I hoped you'd talk some sense into me."

"I'll follow you anywhere, sweet one." He held her gaze as long as he could. A foolish part of him was afraid she might disappear should he blink.

"Fine, but I hope you didn't exert yourself lifting me over here. We'll need your Wisdom for this." She stepped over the dais, twirling to a halt on the other side.

Varka stumbled, steadying himself with Wisdom so he wouldn't bump into her. "Why I'd love to dance, Miss Everbeam, but I think we'd better keep to the task at hand."

"Oh shut up. And don't call me that." Vex gestured towards the tiled mosaic between their feet. "There is a vault below us. Use your Wisdom and open it."

"That's what you needed me for?" Varka crouched down, running his fingers over the little tiles. "You could have charmed any of your puppets from the great hall into opening this thing for us. But seeing as I'm at your command, I'll take a look." Varka sent a cursory probe of Wisdom over the surface of the dais, inspecting for faults and patterns. The grin melted from his face as he realized each individual tile was a separate button. There were hundreds of them. He returned his gaze to Vex, unable to hide his apprehension. "It feels tremendously complex."

"From my questioning upstairs I learned this vault requires each of the three arch priests to open. Collectively they know the combination, but individually they only know a third of the code. The arch priests are too well guarded, and the opening of the vault requires a lengthy ceremony with lots of spectators. I don't have the time to kill all those witnesses and outrun your guild. That's why I have you here," she said, beaming at him.

"That's the only reason huh?" Varka chided, drumming his fingers on the mosaic. "So I suppose you'll have to kill me after. Keep the job clean right?"

"Just get to it already." Her composure faltered somewhat as she glanced back at the doors. "There's no telling how long we have."

"Hopefully this doesn't take me all night then." Varka reached for his Wisdom, bringing it to his hands. Jade light shimmered from his fingertips as he delved into the mechanism with tendrils of thought. After less than a minute of probing he dismissed the magic and stood. "It's impossible."

"What do you mean?" Brow scrunching with worry, Vex crouched low and set her hand on the tiles. "How difficult is it?"

"It's not difficult. It's impossible," Varka repeated.

Vex waved her hand as though batting at a fly. "Nothing's impossible. There's always a way, even if we have to go kidnap the arch priests and drag them in here."

Varka shook his head. "This is the most complex machine I've ever encountered. There's at least a thousand tumblers linked to the tiles, which seem to act as tuning forks. They're all connected by some sort of harmonic relay to a resonator deeper down. This isn't just a vault. It's an instrument." He removed his dagger from his robes and struck a tile with the pommel. A deep bell gonged under their feet. "It would be quicker to initiate ourselves with the church and rise to the exalted rank of arch priest."

Pacing, Vex searched the ground for answers. "Can you break it? There must be some weak point, some sort of vulnerability. Even a class-five vault can be cracked if you take it apart from the inside out."

"True enough. But like I said, this is no vault," Varka waved his hand towards one of the shrines. A shining lump flew across the chamber, slapping into his palm. He tossed the item to Vex. "Do you know what that is?"

She held the inky black gem up to the light. Rusty shafts of light bled through the center, painting her face in ruddy hues. Out of reflex she stuffed the nugget into a pocket. "No, but I assume it's worth a great sum."

"That's Morthainian glass. It's stronger than any other material born of this world. Properly refined, the glass has a myriad of uses ranging from weapons to electrical components." He tapped the dagger on the dais. "Every tumbler, cog, cam, and tube of this instrument is made of Morthainian glass. I've not the skill with Wisdom or mundane tools to defeat such a thing. This task is impossible."

Her pale-blue glistened into his. A sad smile spread over her face. "Did we just fail our first job together?"

"I'm afraid so, sweet one," Varka said.

Vex sighed. "Guess we'll have to see your guild for a *legitimate* job then. I'm more disheartened than I ought to be, but I wanted our first job to be our own. It was supposed to be special."

"I believe anything we do together will be special," Varka said in a soft tone, throwing an arm around her shoulder. She leaned her head against his and together they walked back towards the chamber doors. Varka let out a quiet chuckle. "Now that this job's a wash, I don't suppose you'd care to share what we were after?"

Vex shook her head. "It's a lot to explain. I should have told you on the Ecstasy."

"Indulge me," Varka said, giving her a gentle squeeze.

She slowed, bringing them to a halt just inside the doors. "It's a library. The entire dais comes up, revealing shelves full of ancient texts. Aeneria has been our home since the beginning of time, but there are certain questions that not even our oldest scholars can answer. This library catalogues the origins of Aeneria itself."

This was certainly not the treasure Varka had expected. He wasn't entirely sure if he believed her. It may have been true that the scholars Vex *knew of* couldn't explain life's mysteries, but that was not true of the followers of Wisdom. His home village had been full of Wisdom followers, each dedicated for generations to understanding the unknown. What could this library tell him that he didn't already know? What could be worth all this trouble?

"Vex, where I'm from," he started, trying to find the most delicate way to put it. "My village is governed by Wisdom, not emotion. Though it may be a colorless utopia, the society flourishes in one area; understanding the world around us. There are very few secrets of this world that I do not already know."

Vex withdrew slightly, crossing her arms. "Tell me then, oh wise one, where did your ancestors come from?"

"From Brahdika. It's a series of mountain tribes on the Dark Side," Varka replied, returning her derisive grin with one of his own.

"And how far back can you trace your lineage? To what villages exactly?" she demanded, sucking on the inside of her lip.

"The last two generations were still alive before my exile. My oldest grandmother was a little over one hundred cycles. Before that our records show that my ancestors were nomadic. We had no home." Varka could tell his answer was expected, as Vex's amused expression only deepened. "Does my ancestry seem funny to you? Where do *your* kin hail from?"

She looked past him, her gaze traveling beyond the chamber. "A town on the Dark Side, not unlike yours. We were also born of magic, though Passion extends our lives indefinitely. Like your village, we can only trace our lineage back a few generations before things get fuzzy. The time before remembered time remains a mystery to us. Our most elite paleontologists and archaeologists can't find a single artifact or fossil older than a thousand cycles. It's as if we were simply plucked from the aethers and scattered like seed."

Varka could feel his logic rising up to the challenge. "Just because our ancestors didn't think to keep a journal doesn't mean that we were cultivated by some divine gardener. Also, I don't see what credibility this library would hold, not when its caretakers mutter to the sky for answers while extorting from the poor. I seriously doubt this library will explain much more than theological ramblings. What questions do you think this library will answer for you?"

"Take your pick." She counted off her fingers as she began rattling off questions: "Why does Aeneria repeat the same cycle over and over, and why can't we interact with the local planets? Where does Aeneria exist when it's in-between worlds? What manner of creature are the soul flies? Our telescopes show which planet the Underkin came from, but how did they arrive on Aeneria in the first place? Why is it that only people who have been exposed to Oberon's light breed magic users?"

"Okay, okay," Varka patted the air. "You've made your point. But that still doesn't explain why I should believe anything in a library run by zealots. Religion inherently defies the truth. Why should this doggerel be any different?"

A shadow fell over Vex as her voice became very quiet. "One cycle ago, my town was ruined. Destroyed by some kind of giant…monster. We were all Passion-followers, with no standing army or even a police force, not that it would have mattered. It happened during one mid-cycle solstice. The entire population was gathered in at the central gardens when it came. It was twice as tall as our largest building. Its body…its body was made of other bodies. Dead ones. It was the worst thing I've ever smelled. Almost everyone I know was eaten by the thing, including my family."

"I'm so sorry, Vex," Varka muttered. Her story took the breath right from him. Aeneria had some fearsome creatures on every corner, but whatever this monster was sounded like it was bred from nightmares. More disturbing still was Varka's own memories, which began squirming out of the holes he'd buried them in long ago. With a twitch, he pushed them back down.

"Don't be sorry," she said, standing a little taller. "The event showed me the true nature of our world. Whoever created that monster did so with magic. It had followers too. Men and women in grey robes, casting magic that infected us with a crippling sorrow. We couldn't even run away. I just sat there wallowing while my older sister was maimed right in front of me. I could have healed her, but my Passion was gone. The event showed me there were other magics in the world, and I've been scouring minds all over Aeneria ever since. Every clue has brought me here, to the Stratus Temple. I want to know where that monster's magic came from so I can kill it. This library has those answers. The church hides them here because the knowledge threatens their sovereignty."

Varka's heart was thrumming now. Phantom memories swam forth from the deepest reaches of his mind, wailing as they tried to drag him into their filth. His legs shook as his skin flushed blazing hot. The acid in his stomach churned as his vision shrank to a small, dim circle, as though his body didn't know if it wanted to vomit or faint. Just when he thought he would do both, something snapped to life within Varka's core. It was a little flame, made from the red magic. The flame roared, swelling as it lashed out at the foulness. This wasn't a time for sorrow and dread, this was a time for fire and fury.

His faculties returned to him, galvanized by the red magic. Without a word, Varka stormed off towards the dais.

"What are you doing?" Vex hissed after him. "What's wrong, Varka?"

"I'm cracking this thing open," Varka called over his shoulder.

"But how? I thought you said you couldn't break the glass," she replied, trotting after him.

"With Wisdom I can't. There is another magic within me. You felt it when we first initiated our link," he said, giving her a sobering glare.

"I, I felt something in you for a moment. It was fleeting, but terrible." She leaned closer, seeming more intrigued than afraid. "What is it called?"

"I don't know what it's called. I only know that it destroys everything and anything around me." Varka snapped his arm up, clasping her shoulder. Vex let out a squeaking breath, but did not retreat. "I need you to keep the link open between us. I'm going to try and uncork the smallest amount of the magic I can. Just enough to break through to the library. If at any moment you sense me losing control then you must flee here as fast as you can. Don't stop for anything. Get back to the Ecstasy and leave me."

Varka had expected her to refuse, or argue at the very least. Instead, she drew her hand up to his, squeezing it.

"Okay." She offered him the single word directly to his mind, embellishing it with her solemn promise. There were layers of dread beneath the promise, but they were outshined by her yearning desire for the answers that lay beneath their feet.

Her face became an emotionless mask as she strode back to the doors, halting before them. She rested her hand on the latch and gave him a nod.

Her voice rang clear in his skull, *"Unleash it."*

CHAPTER 10

BLACK TERROR

Varka released a shuddering breath. A waterfall of hot needles pricked down his neck and back. It had been far too long. A dull aching in his hands and feet swelled to fresh agony laced with a savage pleasure. A deep moan rumbled in his throat, seemingly of its own accord. He didn't need to look down to know that his hands and feet were no longer pale, weak flesh. They were now tools for rending and ripping. His fingers and toes grew thrice their length, hardening and sharpening with the death-dealer's black armor. The shroud crawled up his wrists and ankles as his fury consumed his every thought. The red magic became him. He was wrath incarnate.

"ENOUGH!" Varka roared, throwing coil after coil over the red magic, halting it with his will. The beast within struggled and kicked against him, demanding more. Varka twitched, resisting a ferocious urge to cleave every pillar in the chamber. From somewhere under the maelstrom he felt a presence clinging to him. It weathered his onslaught, but only just.

"Varka! Are you in control? Varka answer me!"

Shaking from head to bladed toe, Varka turned to look at her. He couldn't quite remember who she was, but then again he didn't have to. She would break for him, then he would bring this entire chamber down. His claws thickened and stretched as the black armor crawled its way up his arms and thighs. He closed his eyes, shaking and savoring the sweet pain of the transformation.

"Varka!"

A hand closed over his cheek. The stupid girl right in front of him. Her soft skin glistening, weak and waiting. The red magic surged, filling him with violent need. He couldn't take it anymore. She would be his first outlet.

Before he could turn his desire into action, something immense rushed into his face from the girl's hand. He pulled away, only to realize he didn't want to. The power was soothing. It filled him from the inside out with something so wholesome that not even the red magic could ignore it. As the power cooled him, Varka felt a measure of control over his wrath. Pieces fell into place and his clarity of mind returned to him. The beast within was still there, as were his claws and black armor, but now there was purpose. There was Passion.

"Welcome back." Vex gave a weak laugh and released him. She had been crying.

"By the stars! Vex I'm so sorry!" He reached for her, realizing that his hands were still wicked black weapons. "You should have run away! I almost…" He didn't want to say the words out loud.

"Never you mind about *almosts*." She jabbed a finger at the dais. "You have a job to do, so be quick about it. Your little tantrum made an awful racket."

"Right," Varka nodded, inspecting the dragon claws that were his hands and feet. The amount of control he had astounded him. Though the red magic had been tamed, it still burned with unused battle-lust. He needed an outlet. He crouched, flexing his claws as he noticed Vex was still far too close. "Stand behind me."

Vex ran behind a pillar, peeking just one eye out. Satisfied, Varka struck the ground with all his might. Orange sparks accompanied an explosion that made Varka's eyes jiggle. A clean swath of marble and Morthainian glass had been cut from the dais. Chunks of material struck one of the shrines, shattering various trinkets and statues.

"Admire it later! We don't have much time!" Vex's voice echoed through the chamber.

Ears ringing, Varka attempted to muffle them with Wisdom; however, the green magic was too fuzzy among the chaos. He could call more of the red magic and let the shroud cover his ears, but then he would most certainly lose control.

Taking a deep breath, Varka cleaved at the dais again and again, working his way around in a wide circle. The clamor intensified as he worked. Intricate pieces and thick hunks of glass came apart for him. If he weren't enjoying it so much he might have been afraid of the noise he made. Varka continued down, cleaving layer after layer from the instrument. The red magic not only bolstered his strength many times over, it fueled him long after his body cried for reprieve. The chamber filled with acrid smoke as little fires erupted from some of the instrument's metal alloys. Varka laughed to himself, realizing that with each blow the instrument yielded a different bell tone. This would be the final song for the grand machine.

After a few minutes Varka was waist-deep in rubble. He stopped, leaving the chamber in ringing silence. He was hesitant to remove any more from the surface as he knew the library's contents couldn't be much deeper. But how would he raise the library? The controls to activate the lift were scattered throughout the chamber.

Vex's footsteps echoed near as she navigated the debris. She stood above his hole, looking down at him. "Why did you stop?"

"If I go any deeper I risk damaging whatever's in there," he said, stomping out a small fire. "And the controls to raise the machine are no longer useful."

Vex scanned the rubble as she wafted the smoke from her face. Then her eyes lit with an idea. "Well, strength got you this far. Pick the damned thing up."

"Pick it up?" Varka shrugged. "Do you have any idea how much something like this would weigh? The material I just removed probably outweighs the Ecstasy."

"And you just scooped it up as easily as I could shovel a light snow. Pick it up," she repeated, crossing her arms.

"As you wish," Varka said, shaking his head with disbelief. He cleared a space and found what he hoped was the thickest piece of intact glass. He plunged his bladed hand into it, his claws sinking to the third knuckle. Varka anchored himself, jabbing his other hand and a foot into his carved wall. He knew he was at an awkward position that granted no leverage, but the red magic flared at the challenge. Taking a deep breath of the stinging smoke, Varka heaved.

Nothing whatsoever happened. His strength may have increased many times over, but an object of this magnitude was beyond the power of even a hundred men. He needed more, and the red magic was all too eager to oblige.

"Vex, hold on to me," he pleaded.

She enveloped his mind with Passion. *"I have you"*

The chains snapped loose, releasing the red magic's fury. The black armor crawled over the rest of Varka, covering him from the inside out. The magic surged, commandeering his focus and honing it to a single purpose: The library would rise.

The chamber shook. Dust fell in neat lines joining the smoke from the rubble fires. Varka roared with all his might, threatening to break the very air with the power of his voice. With a thundering crack, the floor jerked, sending a cascade of broken glass up into the air. Inch by inch, the library began to rise.

Feeling a fault crack beneath his claws, Varka flashed his hand into a better position before the glass betrayed him. When the top of the library drew near to the surface of his hole, Varka stepped out onto the dais and dug both hands into the instrument. As he took command of the proper leverage, the titanic cylinder ascended in earnest. It rose, exposing spiral shelves filled with glimmering objects. With a nudging from Vex, Varka altered his hands along the columns of Morthainian glass so as not to destroy the shelves. After a minute of grinding, a series of heavy clicks vibrated the floor, locking the whole structure in place. The library had risen.

Chapter 11

Necessity

Varka tripped on his bladed feet, landing flat on his back. With Vex's help he dismissed the red magic, feeling the armored shroud recede from whence it came. He felt as if he'd worked an entire week slinging barrels down at the docks. With the red magic now safely asleep, he felt weak and jittery. He threw an arm up so Vex could help him to his feet; however, she continued past him towards the library-pillar.

"Incredible," she breathed.

"What is it?" Varka grunted, hoisting himself up onto his elbows. "Those don't look like books."

Spiraling up the length of the pillar was a series of shelves containing thousands of glass eggs. Varka brought himself to his feet with fuzzy Wisdom, floating himself next to Vex. His doubted his legs could support him now. He leaned close to the shelf, his nose nearly touching the glowing orbs. Each egg was made from a clear glass, but the insides were filled with thick smoke of various colors. One egg was blood-orange and swirled as if it had just been run through a blender, while another billowed in hues of lazy peach and yellow.

"Have you ever seen anything of the sort?" Vex asked and before Varka could stop her, plucked a churning fuchsia orb from the shelf.

A klaxon wail rang through the chamber, repeating in three short blasts.

"Oh you're kidding me," Vex hollered over the alarm. "You nearly bring the temple down on our heads and *now* the alarm goes off."

Varka snapped his head to the doors. In between the blasts of the alarm he could hear voices and footsteps just outside. "I can barely walk, let alone do battle with the temple guards. We must act. Now."

"Let me deal with them. Just pocket as many of these things as you can," Vex said, stuffing the eggs down her blouse two at a time. Without pausing, she lifted one of her legs and planted a foot gently into Varka's side. "Here. This should steady your legs."

The familiar caress of Vex's Passion flowed into Varka, filling his cold limbs with a delightful warmth. Feeling as if he'd just had a hearty meal and perfect night's sleep, Varka stretched and yawned. He tore his ulrich robes off with a lash of Wisdom, leaving him in his shadow suit and bandoleer. There was no use for disguises now. He pocketed the eggs as fast as his nimble fingers could manage. Angry voices travelled through the door accompanied by a stampede of armored feet. There were two unmistakable pops of gunshot and the doors crashed open. A dozen men in scarlet, plated armor rushed in, their pike-rifles high at the ready.

Varka was already on the move before the first man entered. Wrapped in shadow, he flanked the men as they circled around Vex. Pulling a fistful of sleeping powder from a pocket in his bandoleer, Varka conjured a swirling river of air.

He urged Vex to stay put. *"Hold tight. They'll be asleep in a minute."* Vex did not answer, however; a deathly quiet bled through from her side of the link.

"Drop the cyphers or take your last!" a guard cried, taking a step forward and jabbing his pike-rifle at Vex. "That's a good Cardinal. Now keep your hands where I can see them."

Vex turned slowly on the spot. Her hands were certainly within sight of the guards, but her palms were pointed right at them, as if she were aiming weapons of her own. She tilted her head as a dark smile carved across her face. Her hands pulsed with lavender light.

Varka hadn't the slightest idea what sort of Passion she was concocting, but he didn't like the tone of thought that echoed through their link. He rushed his little river of air along, sending a twirling stream of sleeping powder into the noses of two of the guards. The two men immediately began to sway on the spot.

"What's this trickery?" the guard barked, pointing the long blade of his rifle to Vex's palms. "Step away from the library with those!"

Seeing that she wasn't moving, he motioned to another guard, sending her around Vex's back side.

Her hands fumbled over her rifle with the clumsiness of a person who had never drawn a weapon outside of training. Her eyes were wide and her face pale. After scanning Vex's back side, she called over her shoulder, keeping her pike-rifle locked and ready. "Don't know what that business with her hands is all about, but she's unarmed, Captain."

The captain jabbed his weapon. "Karical, Baracus, get in there and tie her up."

A clanging of metal plates crashed through the chamber. The captain pulled his eyes from Vex to see two of his formation crumple in snoring heaps. His expression flashed from annoyance to mortal terror when he beheld the rest of his unit. Every pike-rifle was trained not at Vex, but at his guards.

"That's it, hold them there, Vex." Varka split his currents of sleeping powder, branching them off to four more guards.

"What in the bloody starlight?" the captain breathed, lowering his pike rifle to the marble floor with a metallic *tink.* He shook his head as his face twisted with bewildered fury. "Lower your-"

A chorus of explosions jarred the air, which filled with a cloud of heavy grey smoke. Before Varka could sort out what the noise was, the rest of the guards clanged to the floor.

"No!" The captain's voice cracked as he removed his helmet. His face was smooth and young. He blinked rapidly as his eyes jumped from each of his fallen comrades. "I-I don't understand." He muttered, blinking faster still, "Why, w-what would...I can't-"

"Vex don't!" Varka roared. Shadows fell from him as he lunged for the young captain.

A blade smacked into the side of the boy's neck. Face expressionless, Vex clapped a hand over his forehead and yanked the dagger forward. Varka fell to his knees mid-stride as the boy dropped to the floor. Spinning the dagger in her hand, Vex strode over to the two snoring guards.

Revulsion fueled Varka's instinct and he shot a bolt of emerald Wisdom at Vex, lifting her off her feet as she kicked helplessly in midair. He wrapped his Wisdom over her entire body, squeezing and immobilizing her entirely.

"Why?" he demanded, his voice shaking somewhere between horror and madness.

"Release me, Varka. You're not thinking clearly and we haven't much time." Her voice was deathly soft. Varka could feel her Passion worming its way through the cracks of his Wisdom, only to recoil as it was scalded by the red magic. She sighed. "Varka, you need to decide right now what direction your life will take. We can palaver over thieves' ethics for as long as you like, but now is not the time. More guards are coming, and they will not be as green as these ceremonial puppets."

Options ran through Varka's mind in quick succession, more than a few of which resulted in leaving Vex bound in the chamber while he escaped. He could feel her watching through the link, though he hid nothing from her. He wanted her to know that her life was in his hands.

After a moment's deliberation, Varka cursed and released his spell. Vex dropped to the floor in a graceful bound.

"We will palaver indeed. Don't you dare touch these two," he snapped, kicking at the two sleeping guards.

"As you wish, but don't expect a warm welcome in Amoskeag for a couple of cycles after these two spin their tales," Vex said in an offhand manner. She swept over to the library and snatched a few more eggs.

Varka shut his eyes and pinched the bridge of his nose. How could she have so little regard for life? These guards may have worked for a crooked church and were probably not even good people, but that was no reason for murder. He wanted to scream at her, to shake her, to make her understand.

As he listed the reasons in his mind, a guilty bubble floated to the surface of his thoughts; Jamarkus, his jailer. While he hadn't killed the man directly, the cannibal in the basement almost certainly had. Varka had let it happen. He could have stopped it. It would have been all too easy to incapacitate the cannibal before leaving his cell, but his lust for treasure had demanded a clean job. At the end of the day he was a still a thief. Hating himself, he stomped over to Vex's side and filled his remaining pockets with the eggs.

Chapter 12

Heist

With their pockets clinking, the two thieves made their escape through the now-empty great hall. Varka had to rely on Vex to lead them to a dark corner near the entrance as it took nearly all his Wisdom to maintain his cloak of shadows on both of them. As Vex had suspected, a second group came in after the ceremonial guards. By sound alone Varka estimated their number at close to one hundred. Their every step portrayed discipline and their eyes scanned high and low for potential threats. After the end of their formation sprinted past, Vex nudged him along. Holding their breath and their clinking pockets, they slipped through the main doors unnoticed.

There was a massive crowd gathered at the foot of the temple stairs, all chattering indignantly over their sudden exile as they loaded into carriages. Vex led them to a dank alley a good ways from the crowds. A silent black carriage slid up next to them as they hustled down the brick sidewalk. Varka gave Vex's arm a gentle squeeze as he dismissed his spells, directing her into the guild carriage.

"The guild docks, driver. We're in a hurry," Varka said, shutting his door and drawing the shades. The faceless driver gave a curt nod and the carriage lunged forward without a sound.

Vex let out a sigh of relief. "I was certain one of the door guards saw us. I dropped one of the eggs right -" Her eyes popped wide as Varka slapped a hand over her mouth.

"The driver might not be real, but the guild has other means of listening to words spoken in their cities," Varka strummed into her mind, withdrawing his hand.

"My apologies. I thought you were too appalled by me to want to communicate in such an intimate way." Her guilt seeped through,

though it was guilt for how she made Varka feel. Her mind held no trace of remorse for the murders.

Varka shut his eyes, peeling back the hardened layers from his mind so Vex could see what lay below. Shimmering with fresh morning dew, his hyacinth reached for the heavens that were his conscious thoughts. Its roots were burrowed deep around his heart. Unwavering ardor emanated from each petal, filling his mind with a sense of wonder and hope for the both of them.

Vex looked up at him, her lips quivering. *"Is…that how you view me?"*

"It is a part of me. What you did back there fills me with a disgust beyond words. If it were anyone but you I would let the red magic decide your fate. But it's you…" Varka withdrew, dropping his gaze. He'd shown her too much.

Vex's fingers curled around his. He looked up to see her giving him that genuine smile he loved so dearly. *"Does this mean you're going to stick around for another job?"*

Varka leaned close, pressing his lips into her ear as he whispered, "I'll follow you anywhere, but I will kill you if you attempt to use your magic like that ever again."

Vex's breathing quickened as her expression became something Varka worried might be Fear. She shut her eyes as an odd desire pulsed through their link. Her terror blended with arousal as her eyes bloomed. Before Varka could ask if she was okay, her hands wrapped around the back of his head, pulling him into a wild kiss. Varka's lips joined hers in a dance of fiery lust, their pockets clinking as their hands wandered.

Vex pulled away too soon, grinning like a wolf. *"Good. I'm going to need your help figuring out what the hell these things are supposed to be anyway. I thought libraries were supposed to house books, not cloudy eggs."* She tapped her fingernail on one of the orbs tucked into her bosom.

"That's easy, sweet one," Varka took her hand again. *"These are called cyphers. I'll show you how they work when we're alone on the Ecstasy."*

"I hope that's not all you show me," Vex said, and flashed a series of tantalizing images through their link. Varka's cheeks glowed through the dim light in the cab.

Blinking himself back to the present, Varka realized all too late that they had passed the guild docks. He leaned forward, rapping on the back of the driver's seat and speaking in a loud, clear voice. "You've gone too far. We're going to the guild docks. The guild docks," he repeated, louder this time.

The driver gave no response whatsoever. Varka was about to grab the hand brake when the driver's white gloves spun the wheel over, shooting them down a narrow road towards the ocean. Tall buildings leaned in from both sides, masking them from Shaskein's low sunlight.

"Where are we going?" Vex's mental whisper was so quiet that Varka barely felt it.

Varka pulled the curtains back. He didn't bother masking the grim recognition on his face, as his dread was apparent through their link. He locked eyes with Vex, speaking in a mental whisper of his own. *"Guild territory."*

Vex's dagger was suddenly in her fist. She shut her eyes, though her head swiveled about. She spoke into Varka's mind in such a rush that the message came through as pure intent. *"Jump out."*

"Don't bother." Varka gripped her wrist with a firm hand. *"If they summoned us, then their eyes have been on us since long before this car picked us up. What are you doing anyway?"* Varka impressed his curiosity at her blind eyes searching the cab.

"Passion allows me to feel the life-song of creatures around me. There's nothing within a quarter mile of us, other than rats and insects." She exposed the spell to him, showing him what she felt.

Varka tingled with the resonating magic. *"I believe you. However, I think we've only just begun treading into deep water. I'm not suggesting we let our guard down, but I think we ought to exercise a bit of etiquette. We would only invite disaster if we ghosted now. Nor should we jump out with blades drawn. For all we know the guild merely wants their cut up-front. Depending on the content of these cyphers, they may be priceless."*

Vex stowed her dagger. The carriage shook with the hollow clunking of tires over the wooden planks of the pier. They were over the water now. The only means of egress would be the narrow passage they were currently bumbling their way down. They were well in the arms of the guild now.

Peering through the front window, Varka recognized the rusty warehouse at the end of the pier. They were not far from the Ecstasy, but without a means of transport their ship may as well be on Oberon. The carriage slowed to a bumpy crawl as it neared the warehouse. There was still no sign of life. Fingers tingling with magic, Varka urged his Wisdom into his ears. He could hear the trusses and bolts creaking with the waves far below, but no heartbeat other than their own. He checked with Vex, be she too could detect nothing. The carriage halted just outside the warehouse.

A whooshing of chains and gears broke the silence as the warehouse wall tilted up, revealing a hidden door wide enough for several cars. The carriage inched forward without a sound, as if pulled in by the shadows themselves. Shafts of amber sunlight poured through the windows like honey. Crates were stacked to the ceiling and the iron shelving was full of burlap bags. The carriage came to a halt in the very center of an empty platform.

Vex's whirring panic sparked into Varka, *"What should we do now?"*

"Be polite and greet our hosts. If they wanted us dead they wouldn't bother carting us all the way out here," he replied, keeping his tone passive.

"Unless they just want to relieve us of these eggs before dropping our corpses off the pier. Has anything like this ever happened to you before?" she asked.

He forced confidence through their link to reassure her before answering, *"No, but we shouldn't make assumptions. Just be polite."* Before she could give thought to another concern, Varka threw open the carriage door and stepped out.

The warehouse looked as if it hadn't been used to store goods in several cycles. Varka's feet crunched over a layer of briny mold that covered every broken crate and pillar. A sour wind, heavy with rotting seaweed moaned up through the gaps in the floor planks. Varka scoured the room one last time with his augmented ears before dismissing the spell. Though he couldn't detect anyone, he could still feel unseen eyes upon him. He would simply have to wait until their hosts chose to reveal themselves. Vex hopped out and joined him, her apprehension leaking freely through their link. She felt like a coiled snake. He winced as he heard the blade of her dagger slide free of its sheath.

"Easy now Cardinal," said a familiar voice. "You're a long way from the temple. Even your ulrich won't be able to protect you out here. Be a good girl and toss that knife, unless you want me to help you find a place to stick it."

A tall figure in purple robes limped out from behind a stack of crates. It was the oaf from the great hall. The floorboards creaked all around as six other priests emerged from the shadows.

Vex relaxed at the sight of the men. Renewed confidence rang through her every word. "You forget your place, priest. I don't know which of the Stratus deities you serve, but you have no business or authority outside the temple walls. Explain yourself at once."

"I believe it is you who has the explaining to do, *Cardinal*." The priest stepped into the light of the sunset. It may have been a trick of the shadows, but Varka thought the priest looked more beast than man, as if one of his parents had mated with a farm animal. "What is a Cardinal doing in a guild car, accompanied by a guild thief, having just completed a job not sanctioned by the guild?" The priest laughed with a grunting snort. "Well, *completed* might be fluffing your tail a bit. Getting caught with your pants down is more like it."

"I…I don't know what you're talking about." Vex faltered as another priest leapt atop the crate nearest her. His nose twitched as he sniffed in their direction. "A Cardinal's business is of no concern to you."

"Your lies betray your shame, Cardinal." The purple robed priest took a step closer as another man skittered alongside him on all fours. "You reek of weakness. You reek of Passion."

"What deity do you serve?" Vex rattled, doing a poor job of concealing her glowing hand. "I'll report you to your head of church if you don't start showing proper deference!"

"Reporting me would do you no good at all," said the priest. "The god I serve is with me always. You'll feel him soon enough yourself."

There was something very wrong with these men. Varka had sharpened his ears to their limits, though their heartbeats, breathing, and footsteps were all hidden to him. He checked with Vex one more time, but her Passion revealed nothing. He would have thought he was staring at a group of phantoms if the smell of wet fur hadn't betrayed their presence.

"Enough!" Varka shouted, lowering Vex's dagger with one hand while exposing his palm with the other. "You caught us. We went off the books, I admit that. But so have countless others before us, and they either paid the fine or ate steel. If the guild wanted us dead we wouldn't be having this conversation. So that means the guild wants compensation. Our job may not have been sanctioned but we are more than able to pay the fee as well as the fine, though I won't give you an inch or a coin if you don't show me your credentials. By whose authority have you brought us here?"

A deep voice answered from the rafters above them. "That would be mine."

Varka shielded his eyes as shafts of honeyed light blinded him. A murky figure descended on a wire, landing on the cracked floor planks without a sound. It was the Cold Crow. Varka released his spells. For some reason he felt an ominous unease with using magic around the assassin.

"Sever our link. Do it now." Varka couldn't mask his terror this time.

Vex gave him a significant look before withdrawing from his mind, leaving him in an empty quiet. He had grown accustomed to her embrace and enjoyed feeling her soul react along with his. Hollow loneliness seeped in where their link had been, spreading like chilled oil.

Varka turned to face the assassin, giving her a shallow bow. "Greetings, Cold Crow. I don't believe we've met, though I've seen-"

"I know who you are, Varka-swifthand." The Crow's baritone voice struck him like a frozen boulder. Her gaunt face now looked more like polished skull in the dim light. "You have made quite a name for yourself among the guild. Some would even call you a master of your craft. However, I daresay there would be a few guild-executives most disappointed to find you taking a job off the books. Especially one of this scale. The Stratus Temple, tut tut."

Varka stood tall. He projected a voice that was much more confident than he felt. "Even the best of us are apt to stick a toe over the line every now and again. The trick is making sure you keep the ones who drew that line happy in the end. So how may I be of service to you today, Cold Crow? I assume you are here to collect the guild-fee that I so brazenly neglected?"

"Lucky for you I am not here on guild business," she said, tapping the long spikes strapped to her thighs. "But funnily enough, it just so happens that I *am* here to collect something."

Varka swallowed, forcing his face into a mask of polite interest as the Crow circled around them. "I'm afraid I can't afford your fee if it's beyond what the guild requires. As you likely already know, I arrived in Amoskeag aboard a luxury liner. I offered nearly all of its contents to the guild. Unless you demand the ship itself, you'll have to wait until I get the haul from our temple job appraised."

The Cold Crow stopped next to Vex. Her empty eyes surveyed Vex from head to toe as one might judge meat at a market. Varka felt the red magic snap and growl. The man perched upon the crate sniffed in Vex's direction, his hungry leer raking over her chest. Varka had a sudden urge to let the red magic off the leash, but an overriding instinct told him to keep his magic hidden. There was no telling what the Crow was capable of.

"I am not here for trinkets or treasures." She ran her tongue over her lipless mouth as her face lit with intrigue. "The Cold Crows may cooperate with the guild when we have something to gain; however, we do not serve the guild. We serve far greater powers. Take heart Swifthands, my masters have taken interest in the two of you."

Varka would rather swim back to Galdebreah than have any of the Crow's associates take an interest in him. He was a man of business, but he was sure he wouldn't like whatever offer the Crow was about to make. He would play along however, as he was certain that their lives depended on how well they appeased the assassin. "Then allow me to rephrase my question. How may I be of service to your masters?"

The Cold Crow pulled her featureless mouth into a warped smile, showing the tips of her greying teeth. "That depends on your willingness to explore the darker parts of your soul. You have barely begun to explore the magic that you are capable of."

A drop of chilled sweat raced down the middle of Varka's back. Vex had inched her shoulder into his. "I'm afraid I don't know much about magic, other than children's stories. They say a job done by a good thief will appear as magic to his targets, but of course it's all nonsense. I say the real magic happens when you convince the target that they made off with more than they started with. Secret-brokers are most adept in the art."

"You are a beautiful liar, Varka." The Crow stepped so close to him he could feel her booming voice in his chest. She was half a head taller than him. "But your deception is wasted on me, for I have been molded by the father of lies himself. Your magic has gone unnoticed for some time now. You weave your Wisdom in the faces of not only your victims, but the guild itself. That alone would set you far above any master thief, but you also carry another magic in you. I speak of the magic you used to raise the library. Even now I feel it boiling in your bones, begging for release so that it might tear us all to pieces. Your Rage feels good, does it not?"

Varka faltered, dropping his gaze to the floor. So that's what the red magic was called. Rage. Disarmed, Varka dropped all pretense. "I…yes it does. It always feels good, but it's too much to control. It has cost me dearly in my youth. How do you know of all this?"

The Cold Crow waggled a bony finger. "That information comes at a cost. Accept my offer and join my masters. Help us bring a new age to Aeneria. An age that embraces magic and power without limits."

Intrigued, Varka ignored Vex's fingers pinching at his arm. The Cold Crows no longer seemed like nightmares shrouded in murder and mystique. Varka now looked upon the assassin through a lens of fascination. She must know a great deal about magic, and her masters must know a great deal more. Varka was tired of scrambling in the dark for answers. He wanted a proper education beyond that of his elementary introduction to Wisdom.

"Let's hear the offer then," Varka said, though he felt as if he'd already made up his mind. He was only dimly aware of Vex whispering something into his ear. Brushing her away, he stepped closer to the assassin.

The Crow's voice was no longer boorish and masculine, but seductive and inviting as she opened her arms. Her eyes seemed to pull all the worry and stress from him, leaving his mind weightless and carefree. "My offer is thus: You Varka, will apprentice under me. I will shower you with my grace and wrap you in the sweet love of my masters. I will help you grow into something far greater than yourself. Do not fret for the trappings of your current life. You may return to your guild jobs whenever you please, that is if such mundane tricks still interest you after you've been graced."

"And what of me?" Vex interrupted Varka's pondering. He had forgotten she was in the room. "What if I have no interest in anything you offer?"

"Your interests matter not," the Crow scoffed. Varka couldn't agree more with her. "You are a creature of Passion. Even now I can taste it seeping from your lover's heart. You will come with me to the Dark Side as well, and if you are very lucky you may be of use to my masters in other ways. That's assuming you make it that far. I may decide to take you for myself. Passion does make for a most satisfying meal."

"I'm not going anywhere with you." Vex set a foot back and tightened the grip on her dagger. "I'll kill you if you touch me."

Varka blinked, trying to remember exactly why Vex was important to him. They'd arrived at the Stratus Temple together, but beyond that he couldn't recall what was so special about her. She looked plain and tired, and her every word felt like a whining needle to his ears. How could he have found a face like that attractive? Anyone stupid enough to tempt a guild assassin deserved whatever fate they sowed. He owed her nothing.

"Oh you won't die my dear. That would be an appalling waste of resources." The Crow's fingers twitched closer to the long spikes strapped to her thighs. "I am very precise. And please stop squandering your Passion on my priests. They are quite immune and I'd rather have you full." The assassin grinned, sliding one of the spikes free.

A shimmering wire flowed from the bundle around the Crow's hips, attaching itself to the base of the spike.

A warning alarm rang through Varka's mind, snapping him from his reverie. The Cold Crow had used unknown magic against him. Varka took a sweep of his mind, isolating each taint as they commandeered his thoughts. Somewhere close to his hyacinth was a growing fire of Hatred, its acrid smoke choking and rising into a cloud of Despair that blanketed all. Roaring through the darkness was a Hunger tempting him deeper into the madness. Steeling himself, Varka shoved the Cold Crow's influence from his mind, but the foulness held fast, sinking its claw of Fear into the fabric of his soul. Unaware of having closed them, Varka opened his eyes to see a metal spike flash before him. He dove for Vex, but he was too late. The spike had found her flesh.

CHAPTER 13

HER PAIN

Varka's spells failed to ignite. He couldn't stop the spike. The Fear that rooted him to the spot had filled his Wisdom with frigid terror. He couldn't move.

Vex brought a trembling hand to her shoulder. A thin wire dangled from a bloody hole in her dress. The spike was buried to the base, her affected arm hanging limp and useless. The curled wire bounced with her breathing, its other end anchored to a device on the Crow's belt.

The confusion on Vex's face changed to a focused calm as her uninjured hand balled into a fist of vibrant magenta. She thrust the magic above her head, sending a barrage of stars swirling above their heads. A warm breeze filled the warehouse, rattling the windows as the stars shot down in a hail of Passion, striking the Cold Crow and each of the priests. Varka felt his hair stand on end as the taint in his mind lifted. The priests all fell to the creaky planks, convulsing and twitching in violent seizures. Vex wrapped her hand around the wire in her shoulder and gave it a timid tug, but the spike wouldn't budge.

"That hurt." The Cold Crow raised her chin, her deep voice laced with malice. Her alabaster skin smoked where the magic had struck her. "We shall see what other fruits your Passion can bear. You my dear are going to dance before you breathe your last. Oh how you will dance."

Horror blossomed on Vex's face as the Crow's fingers whipped over her thighs once more. Three more wired spikes whistled through the air. Varka's Wisdom fizzled useless in a puddle of Fear as he watched the spikes smack into Vex. One hit her other shoulder and the other two buried themselves deep into her shins.

Vex crumpled to her knees, wailing. Her cries shook Varka to his core, rousing the red magic from its stupor. The Rage ignited, immolating his mind with a fire so hot that even the Cold Crow recoiled from him. She withdrew from his mind before he could sink his own mental claws into her. Varka's eyes rolled as the savage pleasure became him. His hands and feet ached and stretched into ebony claws as the shroud inched its way up his wrists and ankles. He would have her.

Apprehension flashed over the Cold Crow's face. Before he could grasp the full measure of his Rage, the Crow yanked her wires, sending Vex sailing towards her and out of Varka's reach. The Crow twisted Vex around, gripping her throat with one hand as she drove another spike into the center of Vex's chest.

"I see your Rage needs some incentive to behave itself," the Crow sneered, shoving Vex away from her. "Don't worry, the wounds aren't fatal. Not unless I give this little string the slightest tug." She curled her finger around the wire that curled up into Vex's chest. "The shard is tucked in between the chambers of your lover's heart, a very tricky place to be. Left alone she ought to live a bit longer, but like I said, one little tug."

The Cold Crow pulled more slack from the thin cable, which whirred into the device at her belt. Breath fluttering, Vex hobbled closer, her blood spattering softly to the floor planks.

A growl rumbled from Varka's chest as he struggled to keep the Rage from burning like wildfire. He teetered between his unwavering desire to kill and his need to save Vex.

A waxy smile stretched the Cold Crow's lipless mouth as she reveled in his plight. "Release the Rage. Or don't. There are other ways of leashing you, though none of which include a beating heart in your sweet."

Varka took a step forward, his clawed feet gripping and cracking the floor planks as he gnashed his teeth. He longed to sink his claws into the Crow, to rip her ugly head clean from her shoulders, but something else drew his attention. Vex's pale blue eyes begged for his own, pleading for him to find control. Her auburn hair clung to the sweat on her cheeks, framing the Fear etched on her face. She knew she was going to die. From the secret place within his soul, a harsh wind battered his hyacinth. The gust knocked a cluster of petals loose, each falling to him like cannonballs. The Cold Crow's Despair crept in between the lapse of his conscious thoughts, dousing his Rage entirely.

His hands and feet returned to their normal form as he resigned himself to his enemy's mercy. His voice croaked as his eyes fell to the blood tapping onto the floor at Vex's feet. "I am yours, Cold Crow."

The Crow chuckled, rubbing her hands together as she savored Varka's defeat. "Much better. That was a most impressive display. I've never seen such control of Rage, especially not one as hot as yours."

Varka searched his mind for traces of Vex's Passion, trying desperately to reestablish the link so he could comfort her. The Despair was too thick, however, and it sapped the will from his heart. He began to think about his new life, a slave to a sadist whose appetite for suffering seemed to have no limit.

"I'm sorry, Vex," he called into the darkness, his lips working the words silently as he braved the agony in her pale blue eyes.

Vex gave him a slow blink. Tears raced down alongside her nose. Her jaw worked in reply, but the spike in her chest prevented her from taking a breath deep enough for a spoken word.

"That will do." The Cold Crow yanked at the wires attached to Vex's shoulders, bringing her to her knees, moaning through the agony. The Crow indulged in her pain for a moment before bringing her empty eyes to Varka. "As my apprentice, you will do exactly as you are told from here on out. You will ask my permission before acting on your own. Your hesitation will be paid for with your lover's suffering. Your disobedience will cost you her life. Did I say you could look at her?"

With both hands, the Cold Crow yanked at the wires anchored in Vex's shins, taking her legs out from under her. Vex flopped onto her back, unable to draw breath for a proper scream.

Varka gave a hollow sob as he gripped his head and yanked at his hair. Seeing the Crow renew her grip on the wires, he dropped his hands to his sides and set his eyes to the floor at his feet.

"You learn fast. If you're lucky I just might let you dance with her once we take to the seas." The Crow walked around to her priests.

Vex clambered to her hands and knees, crawling after the Crow to keep the wires from going taut. Varka did his best not to watch.

The Cold Crow gave an appraising hum: "Passion used for murder? I appreciate the irony, but I'm afraid you'll both have to carry my things now."

From his periphery Varka watched Vex crawling. She was in no shape to stand, let alone lift anything. "Cold Crow, where are we going?"

The Cold Crow yanked at the wires again, and Vex loosed a whispered scream. Her face met the floor with a hollow clop. The Crow waved a reproachful finger to Varka. "I don't recall granting you leave to ask questions, my apprentice. Perhaps you are not such a quick learner."

Rage prickled down the back of Varka's neck. The black claws seemed to grow on their own. He was moving without realizing he had taken a step. The Crow seemed to be expecting his reaction, however. Her lipless mouth stretched into a gruesome smile as she plucked at the wires like a puppeteer.

Driven by the precise agony, Vex rose shakily to her knees once more. A waterfall of crimson poured out of her nose, meeting the rivers of blood running from her shoulders and shins. The wire attached to her sternum danced into a straight line attached to the Crow's waggling finger. Varka halted, desperately exhaling the Rage before the red magic gained any more ground.

"Oh this is going to be fun." The Cold Crow was nearly shaking with mirth as she watched Varka shake with silent tears. "We have a long journey to the Dark Side. Plenty of opportunities to test your control over the Rage. But time is wasting and we must be off. Grab my things."

Varka ran to a stack of heavy canvas bags piled up in the corner of the warehouse. There were far too many for one trip. Wisdom would have made it all too easy to levitate the lot, but the magic was lost to him. The Cold Crow's shadows of Fear crept into his mind, dousing his Wisdom with rotting terror. The Fear sent a freezing lance through his heart as he realized he'd been staring at the bags for far too long. He heaved as many as he could onto his shoulders before bending low and clamping his teeth around the strap of another. The bags were warm and lumpy. Their straps were already cutting painfully into his shoulders. The bags exuded a moldering smell of something that ought to have been buried weeks ago. He took a tremulous step back towards the Crow, but to his horror he saw Vex hobbling over to the pile. He dropped his gaze to his feet before the Crow could see.

"Pick one up," the Cold Crow snapped as she flipped a switch at her hips, granting the wires a bit of slack.

Vex's chest rose and fell with a series of feathery breaths. Tears ran in solid lines down her nose, joining her blood and mess of wet hair. She crouched and attempted to use her arms, but the limbs merely shook at the shoulder. Spurts of fresh scarlet ran anew from each hole.

Varka felt parts of himself sink into stolid Despair, sapping him of every urge and desire. He feigned an appearance of waiting for orders while watching Vex from the corner of his vision. Breath fluttering like a baby bird, she bent low once more and clamped a bag between her teeth.

"You weren't watching, were you? Answer me truthfully my apprentice," the Crow said with a gravelly voice.

"No, Cold Crow," Varka muttered.

The Crow hummed a deep chuckle. "That's a shame. I'm beginning to acquire a taste for your lover's agony. No matter, I'll sample it again soon enough. Carry those out the door and down the stairs to my boat."

Varka took one heavy step after another, listening to Vex's tortured whimpering and shuffling feet right behind him. They carried the luggage down a winding iron staircase to a rowboat moored under the pier. They dumped the bags, and made their way back up for another trip. Varka took the stairs two at a time, trying to appear as amenable as possible. He reached the bags first, using the solitary moment to rack his mind for a solution. The Fear and Despair mired him, slowing and misdirecting his thoughts before he could forge them into something useful. Hearing Vex hobble her way to the top of the stairs, he hastily snatched the rest of the bags, taking two in his mouth and wrapping one around each foot.

"Drop the bags," the Cold Crow said in a bored voice. Varka threw the bags in a heap, keeping his eyes down all the while. The Crow sighed as she wrenched Vex's legs out from under her. Vex's arms crumpled under her chest as her face crashed into the floor once more. The Crow tugged at her shoulder wires in quick succession, bringing Vex back up to her feet before pulling her legs out again. Varka sobbed as quietly as he could. He stared at the floor through blurry eyes as the Crow repeated the process over and over. When Vex's gasping brought her to the edge of passing out, the Crow brought her black eyes to Varka. "I did not give you permission to run ahead and show off."

The Cold Crow made Vex carry the rest of the bags down while Varka walked just ahead. He trudged up and down the stairs, listening to Vex's choked moans all the while. She couldn't keep this up for long. A small voice whispered up from his Despair. The voice wished for an end. It begged Varka to reach for Vex's center wire. Just a little tug and her suffering would be over. Choking back a sob, he pushed the Despair back into its pit with something that had been growing stronger every minute. It was his Hatred. He Hated himself for getting caught. He Hated himself for loving Vex. He Hated the fact that he'd considered her murder.

After several long trips the bags were settled into the rowboat. Water sloshed up over the edge of the small vessel, soaking the bags. Varka couldn't tell if it was the rocking or the water, but the contents of the luggage seemed to squirm at the chilling splash. Despair had settled so thick within Varka that even his candle of Rage had sputtered into obscurity.

"Start rowing," the Cold Crow demanded once Varka had released the mooring lines.

Varka threw himself at the oars, pumping with all his might through the choppy water. He snuck a glance at Vex. She had finally fallen asleep. Exhausted, she'd curled up in a ball at the Crow's feet. He thanked whatever gods might be listening for her momentary reprieve. The Cold Crow's eyes sharpened. As though she had sensed Varka's relief, she brought a gnarled hand to Vex's wet hair. Ghostly blue tendrils wandered from her fingers, digging their way through Vex's hair. Vex kicked and keened, still asleep. Varka pumped the oars harder still, feeling the Crow's empty grin pierce him through the ocean mist.

While the Cold Crow hadn't told him where he was rowing to, he had a feeling he knew their destination. He kept the nose of the boat aimed at the distant glow of the guild docks, ready to change course at a moment's notice. Varka berated himself in between each stroke. How was it that not one day ago he'd been laughing and lounging on the Ecstasy with Vex? They'd spent hours dancing in the sun and fantasizing over heists. Then there had been moments of revealing intimacy that hinted at something deeper than riches and treasure. They had a future together, and it promised a life that neither of them had ever known. This life would bring safety, companionship, and the long burning fires of a love they truly deserved. Together they would discover themselves as they uncovered the secrets of Aeneria. Within each other they would have a home.

Never in his life would he have imagined he'd get himself caught. Yet here he was, captive to an assassin skilled in foul magics, listening to the careful torture of the woman he loved. Varka had never felt so powerless. His head shook with a silent scream. He had only himself to blame. There were rules every successful thief abided by, and even more that Varka had imposed upon himself. These rules were what had kept him safe and rich, a fact that he'd forgotten in a moment's lusting for a pretty face. With each stroke of the oars he counted off rules he'd broken, mentally branding himself with each one. His lapse in discipline had doomed not only himself, but Vex as well.

Varka's arms sagged and burned. The boat slowed in the choppy water. He checked over his shoulder, dismayed at how far away the Ecstasy still was.

"Use your Rage," the Cold Crow ordered. Waves slapped against the little boat, splashing them all.

"As you wish, Cold Crow," Varka replied. He continued working the oars to little effect. He searched his mind frantically for the red magic's candle, but it was impossible to find in the depths of his Despair. He couldn't even locate the desire to find it.

Varka could feel the Crow's eyes upon the back of his head. "Having trouble? I'd love to help motivate you."

Vex's dreaming moans and kicking feet sounded from behind him, breathing life into his candle of Rage. The red magic sputtered through the Despair, battering itself against the sickening taint. As meager as the candle was, it sent a steady stream of energy to his failing limbs. The rowboat bounded up and over the angry swells with controlled violence. After what felt like no time at all they were moored on the guild docks. Varka had guessed correctly. They were going to leave on the Ecstasy.

Varka recognized the young man that greeted them on their arrival. The guild hand stomped over with a group of hardened dock workers, all carrying themselves with an air of challenge. Upon seeing the Cold Crow, however, the young man quailed and looked to the water, as though he considered jumping in and swimming away. One of his fellows gave him a sharp elbow, snapping him to his senses. He barked a few orders, directing his men to assist the Cold Crow with her bags. Thankfully, the Crow allowed them to help. The sight of the Ecstasy and all her opulence seemed to take Varka and Vex from her thoughts for a moment.

"Up you get, my brawny apprentice." The Crow's boorish voice hit him like a kick in the back. Varka hadn't noticed it happen, but the Despair had pulled him into an unwholesome day dream. The Rage was entirely gone now, leaving him frigid and sick.

"As you wish, Cold Crow," Varka said, struggling to his feet as he hoisted himself up onto the dock.

Vex hadn't received the same courtesy. Varka suppressed a cry as the Crow simply stepped out of the boat, dragging the bundle of wires over her shoulder like a sack of produce. Vex let out a proper scream. Varka bit his lower lip and shut his eyes, wishing he could take the pain for her. He ignored the voices tempting him into ending it all for her.

"Where are we dropping these then?" a dock-hand called over his shoulder. "Want us to hail you a carriage?"

"Stow them on the luxury liner," the Crow said, giving Vex's wires a twist. "Put them in heavy storage."

The supervisor slowed, giving Varka an awkward look as he halted the rest of his crew with a wave of his hand. "Um, sir? Do we have your permission to board? We haven't set foot on her since we took your contribution. Your account's been credited by the way."

Varka could feel the blood draining from his face as he debated how and if he should answer. He brought his eyes to the Cold Crow's feet.

"Sir?" the supervisor asked in a stern voice as he hefted a bag higher on his shoulder. As young as he looked, Varka could tell this was a man who kept to an unwavering professional compass. Unlike himself, this was a man who abided by the rules.

"He is my apprentice." The Cold Crow strode close to the supervisor, who averted his eyes and shrank away slightly. "He belongs to me, which means that this ship is mine as well. Heavy storage, dock-rat."

The supervisor was unfazed by the insult, as he appeared too afraid to hear it. He held his ground with shaky legs as he mustered the courage to speak. His voice was surprisingly calm and steady: "If you'll pardon my lecturing, that's not how the guild operates. We need the owner's permission before boarding his property. This gentleman has paid the guild a generous sum for a sanction on this vessel. By the guild's honor, he is the true owner." The supervisor spoke faster as he talked. His eyes widened and followed the Cold Crow's fingers, which were now caressing a few spikes on her thigh. "Sir, just give me your permission, say the word, hell even a nod will suffice."

Varka barely heard the man. He was focusing entirely on the wire that dangled from Vex's chest. Blood ran down the first loop of the wire. The slack twitched tighter with every twirl of the Crow's finger as she laid her empty gaze upon him.

Fear gripping him, Varka shouted at the young man, "I belong to the Cold Crow! Do as she says or I'll feed you your own liver!" To Varka's astonishment, he felt a sudden clarity through the Crow's embrace. His claws flashed wide before he regained control of the Rage.

The supervisor flinched, blinking rapidly at Varka's now clawless hands, as though he wasn't sure what he'd just seen. "By your leave then, Master Thief." He then bowed out of the way in such a rush that he tripped over a bundle of mooring.

Varka shrank back into himself, bracing for Vex's imminent punishment. The Cold Crow's heavy footsteps drew near. Her finger caught Varka under the chin, bringing his eyes up into her empty pits.

"That was intoxicating. You are brave, my sweet apprentice. I do hope this devotion of yours extends to the bedroom. It has been far too long since I've tasted the will of a strong man. I'm sure your lover won't mind. She'll be right there with us the whole time, a toy to add to the pleasure. Her Passion will fuel our suffering as we transcend our very bodies." She brought her waxen mouth close to Varka's ear, dropping her tone to a husky whisper. "There are schools of magic you have yet to experience, but I sense their songs echoing through the halls of your mind. You cast many shadows, for in your heart and in your mind you are many. Together we will unmake you, and from the ashes I will elevate you."

Her message shook his sense of self, casting his own identity into doubt. Varka shivered as her hot tongue ran up his ear. Among the fetid maelstrom he could feel the Crow nurturing parts of him that he'd never explored. Greedy vines of Hunger sprouted, crawling and rooting themselves through the cracks of his thoughts. The cold puddles of Despair and hanging clouds of Fear were no longer fueled by the Crow, but born of his own suffering. Rising above it all was a Hatred that fed off his every regret. Varka resisted, but he knew his conviction was slipping by the second. These dark pieces of him surged in the madness. They thrived off the mere acknowledgment of their presence, granting him clarity and purpose.

Vex's choked sobs wrenched him back to the present. Varka recoiled from the darkness, turning his head away from the Cold Crow.

"There is no shame in it, my apprentice," the Crow cooed, motioning for him to board the Ecstasy. "Fear, Hunger, Hatred, and Despair. Those are all real parts of you. I merely brought them to the surface for you to see. Do not mourn for your Passion, Rage, and Wisdom. They will still be there when we are through. Come, your fate awaits." She beckoned him towards the Ecstasy again.

Varka wasn't sure what was more potent, his disgust in being shown the worst parts of himself, or the temptation that enticed him. Vex's whimpers grew more desperate, driving his feet towards the Ecstasy.

As he trudged on, the Cold Crow took the opportunity to exact yet more anguish from Vex. Her pale face showed only mild interest as she worked. She yanked one side of Vex's body to the planks while holding the other side aloft. The Crow alternated her weaving, waiting for Vex to compensate for the pattern before changing it. Vex no longer moaned or cried, as the exertions robbed her of the energy to do any more than gasp for air. Varka could only watch from the edges of his vision, stifling his sorrow until he had the permission to cry.

Vex's struggling grew labored and sluggish as Varka stepped onto the gangplank. He could feel the weight of the Crow's heavy footfalls through his legs, but the sounds of Vex's breathing did not follow. She was too far behind. He knew the wire in her chest wouldn't stretch much farther. Varka slowed when he felt the Cold Crow's footsteps halt behind him. An ominous feeling crept up Varka's spine as he forced himself to turn around and look directly at Vex.

"Move your legs, or I'll take those from you as well," the Cold Crow snapped at Vex.

Face twisted in agony, Vex drew herself up to her full height. Her Cardinal's dress was no longer powder blue, but a glossy shade of red wine. The dock behind her was slathered in crimson, looking as though it had just been mopped with buckets of blood. The thin wire buried in her chest was so tight that it looked to be solid. Varka's heart cried out to her, wishing she would just pass out. But they were out of options now. The Cold Crow had them. Even death would be a sweet release from their doom.

"So be it." The Cold Crow loosened two more wired spikes from her thighs. "You are a slattern for suffering."

Vex pulled her split lips into a gruesome smile as her chin rose in defiance. She threw her shoulders back, looking grave yet dignified. Lavender sparks jumped from the wound in her left shoulder as the fingers below twitched to life.

"Don't you dare!" the Crow growled as she dropped the spikes and fumbled at the switches on her wire reels.

The urgency of the moment seemed to crack something loose from Varka's madness. Now was the time to act. Abandoning his senses, he sprinted down the plank. Planting a foot, he jumped clear over the Crow, readying his Rage for action. As he flew through the air his eyes met Vex's. The look on her face told him he was too late. Something was off.

With lavender sparks shooting from her wounds, Vex's revived hand jerked to the wire in her chest. Looking to the sky, she wrenched the spike free in an explosion of flesh and bone. Her eyes rolled as her body went limp. She fell lifeless to the waters below.

CHAPTER 14

FATHOMLESS

Vex's body flowed through the air with the grace of a falling star. Her suffering was finally over. Wires slick with her blood followed her down, blazing in the low sunlight. Varka landed on the gangplank in the exact spot where Vex had stood a second ago. He watched her fall, feeling as though part of him had gone with her. He could still taste the fire and life of their first kiss.

Before her wires could snap taut, the Cold Crow wrapped all five around her hands and jerked violently, tearing the spikes from their wounds. The force of the motion held Vex for just another heartbeat before she smacked into the dark water. There was a foamy splash, then nothing. The water was empty and dark, as though she'd never existed.

Varka realized that the Cold Crow had been speaking to him, but for how long he couldn't guess. The Crow's words were thin and vague, as though half remembered from a dream. Despair fell over his mind like a frozen blanket. He could feel the Crow gnawing her way into his thoughts, but even her black arts were lost in his Despair. Varka was slipping far beneath himself, to his secret garden. The hyacinth greeted him like an old friend.

He couldn't recall when it happened, but the lonely sprig had multiplied into a whole grove of black-velvet hyacinths. Their midnight petals had a center of pale blue, the same color as Vex's eyes. The Despair followed him down, sweeping over the grove like a plague. The flowers smoldered and curled in on themselves, dying before they hit the ground. Varka felt himself killed over and over again as each plant withered. Soon he would only have the memory of her scent, her touch, her laugh. His Vex was gone. Taken from him by his own senseless lust for treasure.

But was it his fault? Did he alone bear the burden of fate? The question festered in him like a scab. He picked at it, trying to pry an answer, though he dreaded what he might find. As the last of the hyacinth gave in to the Despair, an answer swam before him: The Cold Crow. She had done this. He may have broken every one of his rules, but nothing warranted the suffering that Vex had endured. No decent person would extract so much piggish pleasure from the torture of another. No one with a shred of moral fiber would drive someone to take her own life. The Cold Crow was irredeemably evil. There was a sudden and violent shift in his tides of Despair, as though the magic had flinched in pain.

A single hyacinth stood in the middle of the field, rejecting the death around it by its beauty and will. The pale-blue at the center of its petals flushed with a fierce glow, pulsing hotter as red sparks swarmed from it. The darkness thickened and smothered, but it could gain no ground. The Despair recoiled further still as the sparks solidified into torrents of fire. The flower bloomed, defying the darkness with every pulse and petal. The Despair was no longer flinching, but fleeing before the Rage.

Varka returned to the present, a single purpose consuming his every urge and desire: He would kill the Cold Crow. His Rage immolated the Despair as if it were no more substantial than dried cobwebs. Varka was acutely aware of another part rising up alongside the Rage, just as potent, but even more perilous. His Hatred rushed up to greet him for the first time.

The Rage was there to protect him and those he loved. It was the soul's outright defiance against an undue death. The Hatred, however, did not reveal its motives, but rather it consumed his very identity, replacing it with a lust for his enemy's pain.

When he opened his eyes Varka tasted the Fear in the air about the Cold Crow. He reveled in it, indulged in the sweet stink of it. He would take her Fear before he took her life.

"What is this? What are you?" the Crow gasped, hastily winding her wires and readying her spikes. "Release it now, or I'll send you down to swim with your lover."

Varka did not answer. This was not a time for words. This moment belonged to action, to pain and annihilation. He would feed both his Rage and his Hatred, wield them with the authority of the void. He could feel the claws aching with need, as the shroud carved its way up his arms and legs. There was something different about the magic, however. Glowing ruby red, jagged veins of Hatred cut through the ebony shroud. They surged, searing him from the inside out. Unlike the satisfying ache of his Rage, this pain was visceral and self-inflicted. He couldn't stop it because he knew he deserved it. He Hated himself just as he Hated the Cold Crow.

The Crow plucked a spike into each hand, spinning them in blurring circles by her sides. Varka took a step up the plank. Sneering, the Cold Crow launched the spikes at him. They whistled through the air, smacking deep into his stomach where the shroud had not yet reached.

"Careful now, my apprentice." The Crow waggled another spike in front of her face. "There's only one more place I can put the next one."

He was blind with wild power, the Rage urging him onward as the Hatred tormented him with Vex's screams. He knew the wounds were crippling, but at the moment they didn't seem so important. Varka took another step, then another. The Crow looked momentarily confused, but then her face shifted to stoic indifference as she loosed another two spikes. The shroud of Rage and Hatred swept over him in response, wholly enveloping his skin. The spikes clanked harmlessly off his groin. The wires in his stomach were snipped loose by the shroud. They coiled and drifted away in the steady ocean breeze.

Varka broke into a run. He felt the Cold Crow's magic scrabbling at the outskirts of his mind, unable to pierce the unyielding forge of his Rage and Hatred.

Abandoning her attack, the Crow leaped to the main dock, clearing several yards of open water. Her hands flashed like pale lightning as her spikes screamed through the air. They flew not for Varka, but the dock workers whose curiosity had brought them too close. Weaving her arms, she yanked four of the dock hands to the base of the gangplank, placing them between her and Varka.

Satisfied, the Crow darted for the boardwalk, clearing the majority of the dock within a few heartbeats. Varka watched her flee, reveling in the thrill of the moment while his claws demanded blood and bone.

The dock hands had barely gotten to their feet before Varka was upon them. Their hands seemed to move with the slowness of creeping vines as they reached for clubs and daggers. Varka knew they were no threat to him, but they stood between him and his sole purpose for existing. His claws passed through their flesh as though they were made of smoke. They met their death before their hands ever met their weapons.

Digging his feet into the heavy beams, Varka kicked off towards the Crow, who was now at the end of the dock. She glanced back over her shoulder, sprinting faster. Her spikes buzzed through the air once more as she flung two more victims behind her. Varka could have ignored them, but the magic boiled his mind beyond reason. They died even more quickly than the others.

Varka wove his hands through the gore, lashing out with a lightning claw and securing the Crow's wires around his arm. He stuck his bladed feet into the dock beams. The wood cracked beneath him as he yanked the Crow off her feet. Her fine blonde hair snapped forward as she flew back. Flattening his clawed fingers into a single weapon, Varka shot his hand deep into the Cold Crow's back. She twitched like a fish out of water as he swung her around to face him. He could feel her body weakening as death flowed into her, but to his surprise her mouth was pulled into a grey-toothed smile. The Crow's black eyes shone with open adoration.

"Do not be ashamed of your darkness, my dear apprentice." Her voice was barely a whisper, a final kiss before the void's embrace. She then repeated her chilling message from the warehouse, "You cast many shadows, for in your heart and in your mind you are many. Let them become you." Her pale hand reached for him, only to fall limp as her face slackened.

Disarmed, Varka renewed his grip on the Rage and Hatred. The two magics gnashed at each other like dogs, fighting for domination of his soul. Fuming, he opened his bladed hand inside the Crow's chest and closed it around where her heart should be. The Cold Crow's face snapped wide, locked in a silent scream. Varka ripped the writhing organ from her chest, indulging in her pain as the life faded from her eyes. The Crow fell to a heap as her heart offered its final beat.

Varka's Hatred continued to twist him as the two magics burned ever hotter within him. There was no purpose for him now, no output for all this power. With morbid finality, he realized the magic would be his undoing. The fact did not bother him, as he knew there was no other option now. He waited in defeated resignation as the Hatred won over the Rage. The ruby veins in his shroud spread like a virus, scalding him in smoking swaths. He could have fought the dark magic, but what was the point? He had no desire to live in a world where creatures such as the Cold Crow existed. Nor did he care to live in a world without his Vex.

At the thought of her, Varka decided to fill his final moments with the memory of her. The Hatred surged, dropping him to his knees as the ruby shroud consumed his entire body. His organs felt as though they were melting and his brain seemed to harden into stone. His end was near.

Varka dredged up his most cherished memories. He imagined his fingers diving through the wild curls of her auburn hair. He could taste the whiskey upon her lips as they pulled him in. He felt her body against his, curves pressing perfectly into him. Her genuine laugh rose from deep in her belly, ringing in his ears forever more. Her fragrance guided Varka to the deep layers of his mind, to his sacred grove where his love was planted. A lone hyacinth stood among the ruin of his soul, clutching at a single black-velvet petal. Varka pulled the flower close, nourishing it with the fading vestiges of his broken mind.

The act of nurturing the hyacinth brought a change to the storm. The Hatred's potency dwindled, replaced by something he had only felt when linked with Vex. Passion of his very own blossomed in the halls of his mind, granting him the energy and clarity to do what needed to be done.

The shroud of Hatred fell from his skin as he stood to his feet, the broken shroud dropping to the dock in brittle fragments. Guided by his Passion, he ran as fast as he could and dove into the water. Her ghostly figure hung in a cloud of red, frozen like a statue of a dancing angel. Varka cradled her in his arms, calling his Wisdom to carry them both back to the surface. They emerged from the choppy water, bathed in an emerald glow. He carried them to the Ecstasy, alighting upon the deck where they'd first danced in Balmoray's fading sun.

He set her body down, weeping as he inspected her. The wounds gave no hint at a possibility of her survival; however, the Passion told him something was there. Following the vague clues of the magic, he planted his lips on her ice-cold brow, pouring all his love into the kiss. She looked just as frozen and dead as ever. The Passion welled up into his eyes as lavender tears leaped from his cheeks, falling like tiny stars to Vex's face. The motes of light sank into her skin, bringing color and warmth back into the bluing flesh. Guided by subtle hints from the Passion, he directed the magic into his hands, which began to glow the same lavender as his tears. An instinctive desire took control of his hands as they drew themselves over the wound in her chest. Warm air and a sound like wind chimes swirled around him as shafts of rosy light poured from his palms.

The wound in Vex's chest began to shrink. The flesh wove itself back together. He could see her heart pumping just before the hole closed entirely, leaving the skin smooth and unmarred. Varka sobbed with joy, bringing his Passion to her shins and shoulders, healing them a few rapid pulses. Giddy with hope, he bathed her face in the golden light, returning it to its untouched, naked beauty. Varka pulled the Passion back into himself. Saturating his lungs with the magic, he inhaled deeply and secured his lips around hers, filling her with the breath of life. Lashes fluttered against his cheeks as her lips widened into her rare smile.

"My Varka," she whispered.

CHAPTER 15

DREAMS THINNING

A warm breeze sauntered its way through the open windows, as if drawn into the helm by a mild curiosity. Varka closed his eyes and basked in the gentle ocean air, hoping it might wash him clean. The taint of the Cold Crow lingered on him like a rotten garment, dank and soiled. Varka took a hand from the wheel and clutched the lump in his breast pocket, caressing the cypher through his shirt. The single cloudy egg had been the only survivor from their encounter with the Cold Crow. He no longer cared for the contents of the orb. His only concern of late was Vex.

They had been on the open water for a week now. Varka had steered the Ecstasy while Vex recovered in the same cabin he himself had recovered in when she stabbed him so long ago. They were in between waters now, sailing somewhere near the border of the Light and the Dark sides. It had been days since they departed company with Shaskein's sun, but the ocean starlight above was most welcome. Varka had no idea where they were going, though he didn't much care so long as each league brought them farther from danger. As they travelled, Varka thought on what he'd left behind. In the lust of his Rage and Hatred, he had killed several guild members. Honest thieves whose families would stay up all night waiting for their father, son, or husband to come home from his shift. Their murders would place the highest price on Varka's head. Then there were the Cold Crows. Killing one of their own would certainly warrant the direct interest of the whole cabal. Varka's life as he knew it was over. He was navigating the waters of fate without the slightest idea where the stars might lead him.

Setting the wheel lock in place, Varka left the helm to minister to Vex. She had been drifting in and out of a cursed sleep ever since they left the guild docks. Varka had checked on her countless times every day, though each time she faded just a little further from his reach. With his newly unlocked Passion he'd poured his heart into her time and time again, though she'd only come out of her cursed sleep for a few precious moments. Hope wilting, he descended to her cabin once more. His last few visits had yielded nothing but a growing dread that she was lost forever.

Varka nudged the cabin door as quietly as he could, though there was little point in muffling his movements. He found her, resting in the same position he'd left her in hours earlier. Her face was heavy with sleep, looking as though she hadn't the slightest interest in the waking world. With gentle fingers, Varka brushed aside her curtain of auburn hair and cupped his palm to her forehead. He called his Wisdom, moving his glowing hand over every inch of her body as he inspected every muscle, bone, organ and nerve under her supple skin. His Wisdom told him nothing, other than her body was perfect and whole. Even the wounds from the Crow's spikes were gone, as if Amoskeag had never happened.

Dismissing his Wisdom, Varka called instead to his Passion. He was unfamiliar with the magic, but his experimenting had yielded a little facet of understanding with each session. He knew her body was fine physically, so he groped in the darkness to where he last felt the weakening strands of their Passion-link. Pulling her into a tight embrace, Varka felt the Passion rush from him and into the void between them, hoping that some fragment would reach her. After a minute's efforts Vex showed no response whatsoever. He tried again, knowing full well that the attempt was foolhardy. The Ecstasy required Passion to keep its systems running. However, without Vex's link the Passion would not replenish as his Rage or Wisdom would. He needed Passion, or else the Ecstasy would be little more than an untethered buoy. Ignoring the risk, Varka squeezed and poured his Passion into her twice more, wrenching the final ingot of it from the depths of his soul.

Utterly drained, he laid his head on her chest and waited for the tears to stop so he could see her clearly.

"Varka?"

Bolting upright, Varka hastily dried his eyes and found Vex's. She looked weak and drowsy, as though sleep might take her again at any second. A few strands of her soul hummed through their link.

"Vex, sweet one." Varka kissed both her cheeks and her forehead. "How long do you have?"

"I don't know." Her eyes drooped and her voice was froggy. "I'm not entirely sure if I'm awake."

"You are indeed," Varka said before a happy laugh took him. "I thought you were gone forever this time. I've been trying to wake you. Please Vex, teach me more of Passion. I cannot lift the taint that the Crow left inside you. Let me help you."

Vex's eyes wandered lazily about the cabin. Her eyelids sagged as if pulled by anchors. Just when Varka thought they would close forever she looked to him once more. "Tell me a story, Varka."

Varka hid his glower, boring his eyes into the floor instead. Every time he pressed her for answers she would change the subject or drift back to sleep. He squeezed the bedpost and asked, "What kind of story?"

Again, she was long in response. "Tell me a story of your home. On the Dark Side. What are your people like?"

Sighing, Varka resigned himself to answer. The way she gazed at him made him feel as if he were the grandest version of himself that he could ever find. He would have jumped out into the ocean if she asked him to.

"My home is called Borla Dign," he said, keeping his eyes firmly locked into her pale-blues. "It lies upon an island in the middle of the Borla River. Every single member of the town is a Wisdom-follower, or at least they pretend to be. People will ignore or conceal any other magics, even if they barely have an aptitude for Wisdom."

Vex's hand slid from under the blankets, her fingers wrapping snugly around Varka's. "Why would they despise the other magics?"

"The other magics are governed by emotion," Varka said bitterly. "Emotion clouds the mind where a logical application of Wisdom illuminates the clear path."

"Borla Dign must be a peaceful place then." Her face lifted and her voice grew stronger. Varka couldn't remember the last time she'd been this lucid. "If everyone sticks to the facts then no one would disagree. Is it a paradise?"

Varka had to break his eyes from hers before he could speak. Even after all they'd been through, the full weight of her gaze was too much to bear. "It's a utopia, but a bleak one. There's no fire, no flavor to life. Everyone is of the same mind, so there is no variance in reasoning. The entire populace works towards a greater understanding of the universe. They toil every waking hour on the task, yet they take no pleasure in it. Someone could discover a spell that saves lives or invent a machine that propels our research dozens of cycles, yet there is no praise or pride. The achievement is dissected and documented, then added to the collective knowledge of the whole." Varka's tone darkened as his face soured. "The loss of relatives is treated with the same pragmatism, no matter the cause of death. A brother taken by disease, or a mother murdered by wandering raiders, it matters not. The loss is investigated and measured. Then if necessary, your family is issued a replacement. Your own child is seen as nothing more than a component to the great machine. That's what they all are. Machines."

Vex squeezed his hand again, bringing him back to her pale-blue eyes. "I can see why you left. Your soul burns too hot for such a place."

"I didn't leave. I was exiled." Varka could feel the color draining from his face as his sub-self dragged him to where he didn't want to go.

"Thievery?" There was a hint of playfulness in her voice, as if offering him a way out of explaining.

Varka suppressed a shudder, then sighed. He had never told this story, not even to himself in the quiet of a starless night. "Borla Dign was attacked. I was very young. At first we thought the invaders just odd travellers, men and women in heavy cloaks just passing through. Some of them had skin that hung like folded rags and their mouths were far too big, though Aeneria is host to many a queer folk so we thought nothing of it. We welcomed them with open doors and open minds. It wasn't until the first screams that we knew the worst had come to pass. Scant few even knew what a scream meant, as most had never heard the noise. Screams are bred from Fear, an emotion that not even our children pay heed to. Any emotion hinders Wisdom to some degree, though as we learned that day nothing strips a mind of reason like Fear. These monsters wielded the emotion like a weapon to which we had no defense. They ate us alive, swallowed us whole."

Varka remained silent for a while. Giving voice to his memories had stoked them into an overwhelming dream. The cabin faded from view as the metallic streets and green lanterns of Borla Dign solidified before his eyes. It was difficult to see through the clouds of stinging flies, though the coppery smell of blood guided him like a grisly beacon. He wanted to help, to fight, but his Wisdom slipped from his fingers like a greased fish. So he did the only thing his body would allow; he ran. Varka cut through swarms of flies, vaulting over monsters feasting on his neighbors. Even though the Fear pummeled his senses, a shred of logic told him to stick to the fleeing crowds as his chances of survival were far greater with so many victims. The people around him ran as if they were on fire, but their movements grew sluggish and sloppy as the venom of the stinging flies took its toll. Varka didn't know why, but he was somehow swifter of foot and clearer of mind than the throngs around him. The flies still stung him, but he was unaffected. When one of the frog-mouthed monsters approached, he darted around the nearest person, putting a fresh victim between himself and death. He convinced himself the first victim was an accident driven by desperation, but after the third he knew he was a murderer. He drove on, darting and weaving his way through the slaughter as he made for his home.

A flash of life and fire brought Varka back to the Ecstasy's cabin as a soothing aroma of hyacinth steadied his flailing heart. Vex's song beamed into his soul and Varka found himself pure and safe. Her pale-blues drew him in. He was amazed that he was still capable of feeling such wholesome vigor.

"Stay with me," she strummed a rich tone, vibrating the best parts of his soul.

A chilled hand tickled Varka's heart, though her eyes kept him steady. *"I've never been there, not since it happened. Please, help me get the rest out. I need you to know."*

"I have you," she hummed.

Steeling himself, Varka closed his eyes and leaped back into the shocking waters of his memories. His feet clacked over the metal sidewalk like a dinner bell as more of the beasts closed in. The crowd around him had thinned, making his survival trick increasingly difficult to pull off. The monsters took their time, shuffling alongside them and snatching at the slowest with their stick-like fingers. Varka sprinted on, his logical side thankful that the creatures preferred swallowing their victims head first so that their screams died out all the sooner.

Varka surged on through the jagged memory, dimly aware of Vex riding along with him. With her at his side, he pushed himself forward to the moment he had been dreading every day since it happened.

"I have you." Her Passion welled up inside him, bolstering his dwindling resolve.

Varka pressed his hand into the cold door of his home. It swung freely, granting him the climax of his blooming Fear.

It was too much. His chest filled with crushing terror, drowning him. He swam away from the memory, away from the horror. He gasped, and his eyes snapped open. He was back in the cabin. Vex's hand gripped tightly over his sweaty palms.

"I can't do it," he pleaded.

"Then tell me." Vex's voice was weak again, but soothing all the same.

Varka withdrew to the outskirts of the long-buried horrors, just far enough to paint their final moments with broad strokes.

Twitching, he focused on a swirling knot in the wall boards, anchoring his sanity to it. Varka continued in a steady monotone, "They were piled up in the atrium. Just pieces. Quartered and splayed out over the floor. I could taste them as though their blood had somehow gotten into my mouth. I recognized my sister's tiny dress first, then father's skin tacked to the ceiling. The other pieces could only belong to mother. It seemed to take a lifetime to understand just what I was looking at. There were cloaked people in the room as well, each nursing smaller versions of the monsters that stalked the streets. They cradled the beasts like pets, encouraging them to feed. They noticed me, but didn't seem to care. A woman somehow knew I was the other child of the house. She worked some sort of paralyzing magic over me, saying that I would 'complete the set.' The final dregs of my Wisdom were replaced with Fear. One of the creatures pulled a lump from the pile. I saw my baby sister's face for the last time." Varka's head gave a violent jerk as he redoubled his focus on the patterns in the wood grain.

"How did you escape?" Vex steadied him through their link with another warm blanket of Passion.

Varka wrapped his arms around his ribs, basking in the warmth of her presence. When he was ready, he brought himself back to her pale-blues, feeling as if they were somehow a part of him now. "The red magic took me. I became Rage."

"What happened next?" Vex asked, her voice sounding as though it echoed from another room.

"I only remember brief flashes. Fleeting moments of violence and bloodlust." Varka scratched his chin. "When I came to, the invaders were all dead, but so was most of Borla Dign. Apartments, laboratories, observatories and libraries, all flattened to smoldering rubble. Those few who survived said I was the one who did it all. I was the one who killed the monsters and their magicians, and I was the one who razed the town. I was called to trial immediately."

Vex sat up a little, "But it was you, it was your Rage that saved Borla Dign. What could they possibly accuse you of?"

"The citizens of Borla Dign were ever the accountants, even in the immediate aftermath of our ruin." Varka huffed an empty laugh. "The invaders killed a great score over a few hours, but they were not the immediate threat. I killed an equal number and demolished nearly every building within minutes. Parents are expected to educate and cleanse their children of emotions. Showing aptitude for other magics was a shame that warranted hefty fines or rehabilitation. I had apparently displayed a master's level of the red magic. The remaining citizens calculated my innate risk, and I was exiled the same day."

"That's not fair," Vex said, heat rising in her tone as she shuffled up higher on her pillow. "That's not even logical. You were inexperienced with your Rage. You never had a chance to learn about it, to learn more about yourself. They ought to have seen you as a resource at the very least, a means to defend against future invaders. I won't speak ill of your parents, but I do wish someone ought to have been there to help you understand yourself. The soul has many facets. None of which are evil, though they do need polishing and nourishment lest they rot and ruin the rest. You did not destroy Borla Dign. The invaders only triggered your repressed Rage."

A wholesome sense of security blossomed within Varka. The feeling came not from Vex and their link, but from a place within him that felt more like a forgotten wound. For cycles he'd thought himself the monster. Killing the Cold Crow and the guild workers had solidified that fact like Morthainian glass. Hearing Vex's words lifted his hope from its bottomless pit, granting him a measure of solace and clarity. Laughing, he realized it was his guilt that had wounded him so. His shame had been released.

"I needed to hear that," Varka whispered. "I think I needed to meet you long before the Ecstasy."

Vex gave him a meager smile and chuckle, merely a shade of her mirth. "Oh I don't know, Varka. There's no telling if our meeting earlier would have led to fortune or folly. Look at the trouble we brewed after just one adventure." She laughed again, stronger this time.

Seeing Vex lucid and warm made Varka's own Passion swell, replenishing the magic beyond its previous boundaries as that facet of his soul grew.

A drop of panic fell between the beats of his yearning heart. He had seen her come back to him before, more wholesome and beautiful than ever, but without fail she'd drifted just a little further back into her sleep. Some taint of the Crow still crept through the halls of her mind. He'd tried hunting the malady through their link, chasing and cornering it in an attempt to understand it. However, each time he'd found it, Vex would recoil and sink deeper into her coma. Nor could he ask her about it. Without fail she would withdraw and give into the sleep just moments after the slightest probing. What was it that ailed her?

Another drop of panic crashed against his gut. Varka twitched once more, resigning himself to the cloak of ignorance. He would hold his questions and enjoy the moment.

"Come to me," Vex tempted him.

"But I am here," he replied, skirting around his mound of sorrow before she could see.

"Come into bed with me. I've never been embraced by one who loved me. Give in to the moment, just one more time. Come to me." Her song called to him. It was as thrilling, yet haunting.

Varka obliged, joining her under the sheets. They embraced as only lovers could, holding and squeezing as their limbs wrapped and snugged perfectly as one. Their breath and bodies pulsed to the same rhythm as they wove closer still.

Vex's breath was hot upon his neck. She twisted and pulled at his shirt, snapping the threads at his collar as she hissed a soft moan into his ear. Varka's hands wandered over her blouse. At first he merely rubbed her back in comfort, but her grinding hips urged his fingers to search just a little farther down. He slipped a hand under the lace, indulging in the warm, rolling muscles of her back. Her thighs opened and shifted him into place, granting his trousers the room he needed to fill them. She snaked her feet around him and thrust her loins into his, gyrating in such a manner that he soon ran out of room in his pants. Growling like an animal, she tore the shirt from his chest and pulled his mouth into a kiss hot and deep. They kept their lips locked, breathing as one while they joined their Passion in wild rapture.

A small voice of warning rang in the back of his mind. The voice was scrambling, desperate to hold onto his most vulnerable parts before they were lost forever to their storm. As the lust spread throughout Varka's body, so too did the madness of the moment. As he entered her, their link broadened, connecting the oceans of their souls with a river of Passion. The charging rapids drowned out the voice of warning as Varka cast the best parts of himself into the torrent. With each facet he offered, the cascade of ecstasy surged until he lost himself entirely. There was no telling where the borders of their flesh and souls met. They were one.

CHAPTER 16

THIEF'S FORTUNE

Varka woke, but he was afraid to open his eyes. He dreaded what he'd find lying next to him. But eventually the needs of his body demanded he rise, and so he did. As he'd suspected, Vex had returned to her cursed sleep. Their link was now only a memory. He brushed her hair away from her ear and called her name, jostling her shoulder urgently, but she was gone from him once more.

He fed her with his Passion, transferring a heavy dose. He knew little of the magic, but he knew it would nourish her as food and water would. Resisting the urge to use his Passion to explore her cursed dreams, he tucked Vex in and made for the helm. He would need every bit of his Passion that he could spare to fuel the Ecstasy.

Back in the helm, Varka flipped a lever on the main console. A hole cracked open in the floor, and from it rose the pedestal holding the Passion stone. Diving into his memories of Vex, he willed the magic into the stone. There was a shift in gravity as the Ecstasy rose a dozen feet out of the water, picking up a burst of speed. With a pang of sadness, he thrust the final measure of his Passion into the ship. He was unsure if the magic would replenish itself without Vex, but he knew he had no choice.

Their lovemaking had revealed to Varka just how dire her situation was. He might be able to sustain her body, but the vileness left by the Cold Crow was spreading through her soul like a cancer. What he felt through their link was not the Vex he knew. There was a dark desire growing in the gaps of her familiar parts. The shadow lingered behind every thought and emotion, feeding on the scraps as it spread to every corner of her mind. While so viscerally connected in their lust he'd seen brief glimpses of the shadow. It was the same awful essence he'd been chasing through the halls of her mind for the last week.

Drying his eyes, Varka dismissed the Passion stone and left the helm. Following some vague urge, he wandered his way to the main mast and gazed up its towering length. Far above in between the rippling velvet sails was a crow's nest he had never noticed. Laughing under his breath, he realized he had never checked the crow's nest when clearing the Ecstasy of passengers and crew. There very well may have been a lone sailor up there, still searching for lighthouses and lanterns of other ships.

Taking a steadying breath, Varka summoned his Wisdom. He took another breath, appreciating the simplicity of the logic required for the green magic. He wondered if perhaps Borla Dign had it right after all. Sighing, he focused the Wisdom into tangible concepts. He desired to be in the air, and the magic made it so. His skin and bones tickled as gravity lessened its hold on his physical form. With another nudge, he urged his mass in the direction of his desire. He rose steadily into the air, leaving his emotions behind as his feet left the polished decking of the promenade.

Varka calculated the chances of the nest being empty, only to realize that it didn't matter. He would deal with the developments as they came, no matter what he found. His eyes crested over the banded metal rim of the nest. It was barren, save for a single wooden flask. His feet alighted inside the structure. Though he dismissed his spells, he held fast to his Wisdom. He was not quite ready for his emotions, which still writhed and whined beneath the foundations of his logic.

Leaning against the mast, Varka scooped up the wooden flask and shook it. The bottle sloshed heavy and full. Uncorking it, he took a long pull, embracing the light burn and notes of Dark-Side spices. Keeping tight hold of his Wisdom, Varka braced himself for the effects of the liquor, which hit him like an eager tide. Numb warmth fell over his Wisdom like a hot bath, relaxing his logic and allowing creativity to bloom in the gaps.

For a long while Varka merely gazed at the garden of stars above him. He wondered if there were any people out there gazing back, wishing for another soul to help shoulder life's burdens. A streaking meteor flashed across the starry painting, drawing Varka's eyes to the horizon where an azure cloud of soul flies were gathered in a coalescing mass. Varka took another pull from the flask, watching as the soul flies shifted to a riot of amethyst, then a rich trove of amber. Then by some unseen command, the symphony of lights shot over the horizon to the Dark Side, where Oberon's glow waited for them just beyond.

The glass egg in Varka's pocket felt suddenly heavy upon his chest. He hugged it in his hands as a powerful curiosity stole through him. A possibility that he had been ignoring all along illuminated itself. The Light Side was not a place of magic, yet even without Oberon's warmth magic had found a way to spill over. He'd left the Dark Side knowing of Wisdom and the precursors of Rage, but life had shown him the wonders of Passion. Then there was the horrible mysteries of the nefarious arts. Vex was plagued by a magic that not only eluded Varka's understanding, but threatened to change her into something that would spoil her soul beyond repair. Magic came from the Dark Side, and that's where Varka would find his answers. Commanding his Wisdom, Varka hopped out of the crow's nest and floated his way back to the helm.

• • • •

Vex's health fluctuated over the next week. Some days Varka could rouse her enough to walk the promenade, though most days he couldn't get her to open her eyes. Once again his Wisdom showed that her body was whole and healthy, though his Passion was too fickle to reveal the ailments of her soul. Varka took her good days when they came, and on her bad days he worked tirelessly over the Ecstasy. Sails and ropes began to fray in the lashing wind, and thousands of bolts wriggled themselves loose from the ship's sprints. The Ecstasy was easy enough to pilot with one man, but the maintenance required a whole team. Without Varka's Wisdom aiding him with the repairs, the ship wouldn't have lasted another week. Most demanding of all was the Passion stone, which powered the ship's life utility systems and kept the hull flying safely above the water. The Passion stone required daily filling, but to fill it Varka needed Vex and their link.

One day, when Varka felt Vex was strong enough, he carried her to the helm and showed her the star charts. He concealed his intentions as he hefted her along, as she seemed only interested in sex during her waking hours. Varka cherished the moments when she was awake as lusting with her was the best thing he'd ever felt, but it was not sustainable. Varka could no longer replenish his Passion fast enough to keep the Ecstasy aloft, and their journey would take longer than their supplies would last.

"Where are we?" Vex asked as Varka set her down in the captain's seat. She peered out the window, her dreamy eyes widening with awe. "Is that Oberon?"

Varka wrapped a blanket around her, tucking it around the seat so she wouldn't fall out. "We are in a safe place, sweet one. And yes, that is our moon."

Floating half-exposed upon the horizon was Oberon, Aeneria's moon. The old sentinel was as big as a dinner plate held at arm's length. Its pocked surface bloomed and swirled with explosions of ever-changing hues, as though it couldn't decide what color it wanted to be.

"But why?" Vex asked, keeping her eyes on Oberon. "Varka I don't want to go back. I can't go back. My home is on the Light Side."

"Your home is with *me*, sweet one." Varka caressed her cheek. "As long as we have each other we can go anywhere. The world is open to us so long as we are open to each other."

Vex dropped her eyes. Her breathing slowed as her face drooped. Varka cupped his hand around her head and thrust a precious fraction of his remaining Passion. He wouldn't let her sleep. Not until she gave him just a little help. Her face lifted somewhat, though her eyes looked as though she would rather be somewhere else.

"Stay with me now, sweet." Varka took his hand back, but held on tight to their link. "That evil witch left some sort of foul magic in you. I can feel it in there, writhing and rotting more and more every day. I've tried everything in my power to heal you, but I'm at a loss. I'm confident Wisdom is not your answer, and neither is Rage. That leaves Passion, or some other magic that I've yet to learn. Seeing as you won't teach me any more of your Passion, we must return to the Dark

Side for answers before this taint destroys you. Unless you care to tell me what ails you? What are you feeling right now?"

Varka could feel her consciousness slipping, but he had learned enough of Passion to hold her awake just a little longer. Sagging against his mental embrace, she brought her pale-blues to him. "I don't know. I can't describe it."

"Try," Varka pleaded. "Just try. Sometimes it feels as if you're not even fighting it, like you don't care if it takes you. I don't want to lose you, Vex. You are a part of me now."

She was silent for a full minute, her eyes boring unseeing and uncaring through the floor of the helm. Eventually she blinked and spoke in a weak voice. "I don't know."

Rage flushed up into Varka's cheeks, but he stifled the magic, instead pouring more of his Passion into her. "You're not trying."

Vex stirred in her cocoon of blankets, wrapping them tighter around her as she turned her head towards Oberon. "Release me. Passion is not meant to be used as a leash."

Stung, Varka recoiled. His hurt was soon replaced by logic and whispering traces of something darker that bled through their link. "Is that what you think is happening here? I am holding you prisoner?"

"If you disagree then release me." Her face hardened and her eyes turned from pale blue to cold steel.

Varka turned away, swallowing the blow to his heart. "No. You'll hear what I have to say, then I'll release the Passion. I will never initiate our link again. If you want anything to do with me you'll have to make an effort. I'm tired of it." He waited a few seconds to see if his words had any effect, but they did not. Sighing, he continued, "Vex, you are dying. You don't eat or drink, and I'm not sure if your sleep is killing or preserving you. I've been keeping you alive with Passion. The Passion that *you* planted inside *me.*"

With the firm yet gentle grip of the magic, he directed her focus into his mind, showing her the fields of hyacinth rolling and thriving under the starlight. There were thousands, all glistening with droplets made from his own sorrow. Each sprig represented a memory of her, every petal a treasured detail. This was Varka's home.

Returning them both to the darkened helm of the Ecstasy, Varka continued, "Whatever is inside you is killing you faster than my Passion can heal you. I need you, the real you, to help me. Let me save you, Vex. I want to indulge in our life together, but it has to be your want as well. Our supplies will last another week at best, and if we don't fill the Passion stone it will take a month to reach the nearest port. I can no longer fuel the stone without you." Even as he said it, he felt the aching strain maintaining their link ebb away. His Passion sputtered and died. Vex slipped from his mind entirely and their link was replaced by a fragile darkness.

"I have no answers for you, other than I cannot return to the Dark Side. Do not pressure me, Varka. You'll only push me away." Vex sagged in the captain's seat. The strength in her voice dwindled with every word.

Varka bit his lip, unsure if he wanted to scream or weep. Blinking out a hot tear from each eye, he breathed, "Then tell me what it is you want. I'll follow you anywhere, sweet one."

She didn't respond. A flicker of Rage struck at Varka's chest. He ground his teeth and looked her square in the eyes, but she was already back in her cursed sleep. He carried her back down to her cabin, tucking her in with fresh clothes and sheets. He attempted to nourish her with Passion, but the magic was utterly depleted. Quiet as a shadow, Varka left the cabin and made for the crow's nest, where he sobbed himself to sleep.

The food ran out sooner than Varka had estimated, and the drinking water even sooner. A few days of lean rations motivated Varka to craft a few spells with Wisdom to catch fish and purify the sea water. The fish were easy enough to snag as he only had to levitate them to the main deck, though luring them within range was a capricious task. Removing the salt from the ocean water took a far greater effort of Wisdom. Emulating the Ecstasy's own systems, he collected and boiled the sea water with a spell, which took an astonishing amount of energy and focus. Then he cast another spell to convince the steam to move and cool into a bucket, where it returned to a liquid state. The process took hours, leaving him profoundly exhausted, and yielded barely half a day's worth of fresh water.

He wished he had spent more time learning Wisdom in his youth and less time getting into fights and playing with animals.

Since their confrontation in the helm, Vex had not come out of her sleep again. Varka had returned to her night after night, attempting to eke some Passion into her, but the magic eluded him just as she did. She slept a week straight without nourishment of any sort, other than the little water Varka could wet her lips with. With his Wisdom he combed through every fiber in her body, determined to find some clue, but there was none to find. When her ribs and cheek bones started poking through her paling skin, Varka called his creativity to his Wisdom. He cast a spell over Vex, changing the effects of time over her body. As long as she didn't move, time would flow a bit more slowly in the space she occupied. It would only extend her life by another week or so, but it was all he could do. The spell was heavier than Varka had expected, and its toll on Varka's Wisdom took a constant effort of focus. He stumbled around the ship like a drunkard, with barely enough attention to spare for the simplest of tasks. His spells for fishing and making fresh water were now beyond him. Most worrisome of all were the angry clouds gathering around Oberon.

Another week had passed in belabored misery, draining the Ecstasy of the final dregs from the Passion stone. The hull now bobbed and crashed over the waves like a common sloop, propelled solely by whatever fickle winds Varka could enlist to the sails. The distant storm clouds had swallowed Oberon and spread over half the sky, leaving the Ecstasy shrouded in ever thickening darkness.

One day Varka woke from his slumber in the crow's nest to a powerful howling. The wind tossed him about, threatening to tear the sails from the masts. He hobbled around the ship taking in every bit of slack he could find, but the wind redoubled in strength by the end of the day. The sails began to tear at the beating, and so Varka spent the rest of the day securing them tight to the masts. Sometime in the evening a heavy rain accompanied the roaring gusts, breaking Varka's resolve. It was too much for him, especially while he maintained his spell over Vex. With wind tearing the breath from his mouth and rain striking him like stones, Varka retreated to the helm. Vex slept below the rolling hull all the while, never stirring.

Over the following day the clouds swept over the rest of the sky, leaving the Ecstasy in utter darkness. The wind and rain battled each other to a ceaseless crescendo. It was as though each element was hell-bent on breaking the ship before the waves could crack the hull in two. In preparation for the oncoming siege Varka sealed every porthole and door, but despite his efforts, portions of the lower holds began taking on water. The Ecstasy had pumps to evacuate the water, but they'd remained useless so long and the Passion stone was empty. Without the stars or power to the ship's navigation systems, the Ecstasy groped aimlessly through the dark waters. Varka waited out the storm in Vex's cabin, making sure the bucking waves didn't toss her out of bed; however, after what felt like a day the storm seemed to only gain in strength. With a heavy heart Varka released his time-spell over Vex.

With his Wisdom returned Varka focused the magic into his eyes, granting him sight in the darkness. He was weak both in body and mind, but the feeble spell revealed to him the full measure of the Ecstasy's damage.

Of the once-velvety sails there remained no more than flapping strips clinging to the cross beams. The fore and mizzen masts were nowhere to be found, and the main mast rolled like a fallen tree about the promenade. The storm had ripped every structure from the upper decks, leaving a sloshing, blended mess of wood and iron shards.

When the wind yanked the roof of the helm overboard, Varka retreated back to the cabins. There was no longer anything worth saving on the upper decks. The sails, the rudder controls, the masts, as well as every magic-powered system all belonged to the storm.

Varka descended past the cabins and crew's quarters. He cranked open the latch to the lower holds, intending on checking the damage below. A deluge of seawater rushed through and Varka sealed the door with Wisdom. The lower holds were entirely flooded now. It was in this moment that Varka's hope betrayed him entirely, replaced instead by a Despair that had been waiting for such a moment to drag him to its depths. It was as if the Cold Crow had never left his mind, that she had merely left him with a seed of madness which now began to sprout and take root.

At the thought of the Cold Crow, Varka's Rage pulsed like a fiery beacon, burning the Despair away from his core. His Rage was weak and tired, but it was enough to keep him standing. Hope may have abandoned him, but the red magic wasn't ready to give up quite yet.

Holding his Rage like a torch, Varka made his way through the rolling halls to Vex's cabin. He found her fast asleep, somehow still in the bed despite the Ecstasy's violent rocking. She looked entirely at peace. A swath of her wild auburn hair dangled off the side of the bed, swaying with the waves. Varka wished she would open her black petal lashes so he could see her eyes just one more time. Realizing the tips of his fingers were ebony claws, Varka dismissed the Rage and traced his thumb over her forehead and down her cheek. He would save her.

Laying himself flat on the soft carpet, Varka emptied his mind and drew upon his Wisdom. There was no spell for what he was about to attempt, and he knew the drain on his focus might kill him, but he must try. He would not wait for death to come for him. Should death interfere with his pursuit of life, then death would have to prove itself his worthy master before Varka would bend to it. For now, he was going to fight.

When his errant thoughts had ceased their buzzing, Varka embraced his Wisdom. Keeping his eyes closed, he directed his focus to the floor beneath him. His head lolled with the rocking of the ship, but that was fine. The ship would rock, and so would he. With every breath Varka sent a tendril of his own consciousness to the floor beneath him. His mind spread into the posts and beams around the room, still strong and sturdy despite the storm's trauma. He wandered farther out, bypassing the weaker planks and seeping deeper into the heavy timber that was the ship's skeleton. Soon Varka was no longer of his own body. He creaked and groaned as he wrestled the waves crashing into his hull. Parts of him cracked and snapped, but for the most part he was whole and strong. With the smallest fragment that was still safe in his mind, Varka guided the rest of his Wisdom into action. He set a rule over the heavy frame, compelling it with his will.

You will move.

The drain was immediate. His sliver of coherence blurred and swooned. The parts of him that still gripped the Ecstasy's frame threatened to slip away into non-existence, lost to him forever. But somehow, he held on.

You will move.

Varka's focus did not waiver; however, the ship was massive. There was no way of knowing if his efforts had any effect. The forces applied by the mountainous waves and shearing wind threatened to break him with each blow. The task was beyond the will of a single mind, but still he persevered. There was no guessing what direction the Ecstasy went, or if it moved at all, but Varka held on. His fragment of self still within his mind brought Vex to light, fueling the magic needed to battle the elements. He had to save her.

Time had lost all meaning in the ceaseless lurching and pitching. Varka was only dimly aware of the ominous explosions that jolted the frame. Nor did the sensation of cold wetness creeping up his back rouse his interest. He existed mostly within the frame of the Ecstasy: His curiosity, self-preservation, desire, all busy with the herculean task of moving the mass of wood and metal around him. Only when his throat clamped shut and his mouth filled with salty ice did he take notice of his own body. His sliver of self screamed for help, crying out for the rest of his mind. With agonizing slowness, Varka pulled himself piece by piece back into his body.

Panicking, Varka opened his eyes and bolted out of the shallow water. His lungs flared with a heavy, choking pain and his throat wouldn't open. His head and torso were free of the water, but his lungs were not. He was drowning. He grasped his Wisdom and slapped an emerald hand to his chest. As he injected the magic into his lungs, his chest swelled and forced his throat open as a gout of cold steam erupted from his lips. Hacking through the chilled magic, Varka gulped in what precious air he could. Only now did he realize his vision had blanked to black. His field of view slowly opened to him, as though coming out of a tunnel.

A foot of freezing water sloshed about the cabin. Varka was soaked to the bone, his teeth clacking like wooden ratchets. Vex was still asleep. Her arm dangled over the bed, her fingers just a hair from the rising water.

Coughing out the bitter sting of salt, Varka rose to his wobbly feet. He was heavy and feeble. His body relayed a sense of diminishment that could only come from days without nourishment. How long had he been maintaining the spell?

Barely strong enough to walk, Varka splashed his way over to Vex, drawing upon his Rage to grant him the energy needed. His Rage was silent, however. He could feel it within him, but calling it was like trying to start a fire under water. He called instead to his Wisdom, but it too was beyond his reach. His Passion had long been of no use to him. His body and mind had been pushed long past their limits, and they were now failing him. Varka was eroding from the inside out.

An echo of hope fluttered out from between his pruned lips, carried by the breath of a hollow sob. Crouching, Varka wound his arms under Vex's back and knees. Taking advantage of the Ecstasy's rocking, he gripped her clothes and heaved, lifting her before the water could slosh back and soak her hand. Varka hefted her frail form, pulling her head safely into his shoulder. She felt as light as a dried skeleton. Even through her clothes he could feel the stark bumps of her ribs and tendons. He knew she may even have been dead already, as he soon would be.

Leaning against the walls for support, Varka trudged through the rising water to the stairs. He knew death was near, but living one's final moments trapped in a room full of water held no appeal for him. They would brave the storm one last time. Shivering from his bones to his ears, Varka rested his head against the door to the upper deck. He needed a moment to recover. Steeling himself, he held Vex with his knee while stretching his cramping hand towards the latch. His finger had barely touched the brass lever when the door swung free, spilling him and Vex over the upper deck. Too weak to brace himself, Varka dropped Vex as he crumpled against the decking. Something was wrong, however. Varka was struck with a sensation he hadn't felt in what seemed like a lifetime.

A gentle breeze flicked over him, sultry and tropical. Even the harsh grain of the decking felt like a warm massage over his frozen cheek. Varka didn't have to open his eyes to know that the sun would blind him. Were they really out of the storm? Surely his spell hadn't pushed them all the way back to the Light Side. When his vision adjusted, Varka slumped to his hands and knees and cracked his eyes open.

The entire deck was bone dry and scraped clean. There was no trace of rubble, nor remnant of any structure. It was as if some giant had shaved the Ecstasy with a massive cleaver. Varka rose to his knees. He blocked the sunlight with his hand as he peered out to the waters beyond. The storm still warred about them, throwing sheets of thick rain and tossing swells twice the height of the Ecstasy. Yet somehow the ship sat in a neat little ray of warm sunshine and calm water. The hull had sunk more than halfway under the surface, yet the storm's swells curved around them as if repelled by some unseen force. A sudden stirring drew his attention.

"Varka," Vex croaked.

"Vex!" he cried. Falling to his hands, he shuffled over to her, splintering his palms along the way. "Sweet one! You're alive!"

"Am I back on the Light Side? Is it over?" She curled into him, wrapping her arms around his middle.

Overwhelmed with relief, Varka sobbed as he embraced her. He ran his hands fervently over her back, trying to rub some warmth into her icy flesh. He began weeping in earnest. He wanted nothing more than to tell her that it was over, that she was safe and sound. But he couldn't.

"No, sweet one." Varka entwined his fingers through her hair. It was still lush and full, somehow still carrying that aroma of hyacinth. "The Ecstasy is destroyed. There's barely anything left of her now. Don't look, love. You won't recognize her."

"But it's over now. Please tell me it's all over," she said. Her voice was no more than a dry whisper.

Varka didn't want to answer. He wanted Vex to bring her head up and look at him. How he longed to gaze into those pale-blues just one more time. "No, sweet one. We are only in the eye of the storm."

Vex deflated in his arms. Varka tried pulling her head up. If only she would just look at him she would see how he still cared, how he still fought tooth and nail for her. Then perhaps she would re-establish their link. Her Passion would nourish his own and save them both. Vex made no effort, however. She lay under him like a sack of cold sticks.

A powerful female voice broke the silence: "You are not in the eye of a storm, Varka of Borla Dign. You are in *my* eye, however."

Varka's heart forgot to beat. Swallowing his doubts, he slumped up on his elbows, trying to find the mystery woman.

She sat comfortably in a chair not two paces from him. Her clothes were rugged and travel-worn, as if she worked a job as a woods-guide. Her knee-high boots were dirty and adorned with ornate wooden buckles. A heavy brown duster hung over her shoulders, the ragged coattails draping over her crossed legs. A loose bun failed to contain several bundles of flyaways, giving her the appearance of one who had just been electrified. She rested an elbow upon the chair's armrest, cupping her chin in her hand. The woman looked down at Varka with a mixture of contempt and appraisal, as though measuring the worth of a questionable trinket.

"Get yourselves up now," she said, raising her chin a little. "Let me have a proper look at you."

Varka pulled Vex closer. "Good lady, we're not exactly in a condition to stand by our own power." He gestured towards Vex's prone form. "Her least of all. She's been tainted with an evil magic that's been dragging her through death's gardens."

The woman's eyes narrowed as she inspected Vex. "Her state is grave, but it is of her own doing. There is no foreign magic meddling with her at the moment. You've both dug yourselves into a pit, and you'll be the ones to dig yourselves out if you want to live. Now, get up."

Varka was unsure if he should trust this woman. Her snide tone made his blood boil, and he was quite sure she was cycles younger than he. He buried his irritation beneath his desire to save Vex. This woman was their only chance. Grinding his teeth, he dragged himself to his knees, then to a crouched position. He yanked at Vex's shirt, but she might as well have been attached to the ship.

"Stand aside," the woman snapped.

There was a flash of green light and Vex rose to her feet. The mysterious woman had used Wisdom. Vex's eyes bloomed just enough for Varka to get a glimpse of her pale-blues. She remained silent.

"I see you now." The woman spoke in an indulgent cadence, as if she liked how the words tasted. "Quite the unique pair. A matching set, unless I'm mistaken. Aethers take me, it makes perfect sense. The pebbles that caused the ripples of the storm that cripples…" Her voice trailed off as she ran her eyes up and down their gaunt forms.

Varka broke the silence: "Good lady, my friend is dying. Her name is Vex, and I love her more than I love myself. I beg you to help her. I see you are a Wisdom user, and a powerful one at that. Please, help her."

A wry smile pulled at the woman's cheek. "And what would you offer me in exchange for her life? What are you worth, Varka of Borla Dign?"

Varka spoke without hesitation: "I offer my life. From now until the end of my days, I will be yours."

The woman looked from Varka to Vex. She appeared amused, though she showed no sign of intrigue at Varka's offer.

Curiosity itched to the tip of Varka's tongue. "Good lady, what is your name? And how do you know mine?"

The woman pierced Varka with a look that left him feeling vulnerable and exposed, as though he were a child caught in mischief. She held his eyes for far too long before speaking. "My name is Ka Reine, not that it matters. You'll forget my name before your next waking. As for you, Varka of Borla Dign, and you, Vex of Brimhallow Haven, I've been watching you both for some time now. Alone, each of you has created enough disturbance in the aethers that it keeps me from my sleep. Together though, you tilt all of Aeneria off its fulcrum. You are two pebbles dropped into a pond, your ripples matching in exponential synchronicity that will cripple the world. You must be stopped, lest you destroy us all."

"I think you have us mistaken, Ka Reine." Varka kept his voice even, though his legs were ready to collapse. "I assure you, Vex and I have no aspirations to destroy anything. We only want to go about our lives in peace."

Ka Reine threw her head back as her chest rose and fell with haughty laughter. "Come Varka, even you know how far from the truth that is. The two of you are magic users. Rare magic users who have managed to express Rage, Passion, Wisdom, as well as a few of the less-savory arts." She paused with a long sigh, keeping her eyes on Vex. "You are both master thieves, your every breath and whim are spent on taking more than you ever give. For that crime alone common law demands a fate far worse than what I'm going to set upon you."

"What exactly do you have planned?" Vex croaked. Her face was slack though her eyes blazed with rebellious zeal. "If you know of Passion then you know it does not abide Wisdom. You do not have the power to enforce any fate upon me."

Ka Reine chuckled again. "You know nothing of Passion, slattern, at least nothing outside what the burning of your loins has shown you. You'll accept my fate like an offer of flesh to a sex-starved whore. I see you, Vex. Even without my Passion I see you as plain as a cat in heat, mewling and writhing for all the toms to see."

The chill fled from Varka's bones as his Rage finally found a spark. He could feel the satisfying ache stretch his fingers to ebony blades. Ka Reine watched Varka's budding claws with growing interest. She flashed her eyes and the air before her seemed to freeze. Varka felt as if a bell clanged in his skull, shaking every thought and desire from him. His hands had somehow returned to normal.

"I could kill the both of you, right now," Ka Reine warned, waggling a finger at Varka. "But seeing as neither of you has displayed an act of evil, I'll grant you another option."

Varka blinked slowly. He looked to Vex, but her eyes were locked on Ka Reine. If only she would just look at him. Sinking back into Despair, he gazed back to Ka Reine. "Give us your options."

Ka Reine uncrossed her legs with a flourish and rose to her full height. With a casual flick of her boot she sent her chair careening over the edge of the Ecstasy. Bending low, she scooped something from a loose plank under where she'd been sitting. Her duster whipped about her knees as she turned around and hefted a small, cloudy egg in her hand. Varka patted his chest pocket. It was empty.

"Your options are thus." She kept her eyes on Varka while the hand that held the cypher morphed into wicked black claws. "You can stay on your Ecstasy. You will be free to do with your life what you please and you will never see me again. I warn you however, as sure as these waters are deep you will die within a day. This storm was created for you, by you, and it will kill you." She spun the egg between two bladed fingers before tossing it to Varka. It landed keenly in his breast pocket. "Or, you can each board a separate life-boat. The vessels will take you to safety, where each of you will live out your separate lives. The choice is yours to make, though the latter has a price. As soon as the two of you part company, you will each lose all memory of the other. Every moment shared, whether trivial or treasured, will be wiped from your minds."

Her words struck Varka like an avalanche. What right did she have to impose such a fate? There had to be another way.

Ka Reine pressed a palm towards them as the air before her buzzed with unseen magic. Varka's mind slipped and swam, overwhelmed in the currents. He couldn't hope to contend with the spell, let alone understand it. Ka Reine then said something but the words fell from his memory before he could grab them. Varka opened his mouth to protest but the woman was already rising into the air, carried aloft by sweeping emerald wings.

"The choice is yours," she called, and pointed her hands at opposing sides of the ship where two lifeboats were nestled, undamaged and whole.

Varka shielded his eyes as Ka Reine disappeared into the brilliant golden light above them. The storm clouds rushed in around the gap, leaving the Ecstasy in the dark wrath of their eternal squall.

Lunging, Varka caught Vex before her head could strike the decking. Though he could do little more than break her fall, he relished the moment because she was still with him.

"Sweet one, please look at me." He pushed her hair from her forehead. "Do not fret over that woman's lies. I won't let you die. We'll get through this together. Please, just look at me. I need you. I can save us both if you just look into my eyes. Vex, please…"

Vex was already asleep. Varka pulled his thumb gently over her lids, only to gaze at veiny, rolling whites. The Ecstasy gave a sudden, massive lurch. Varka held onto her as they tumbled across the deck. He threw a leg out, and his foot caught on a jagged hole in the deck.

"Please Vex!" Varka roared over the rising wind. "Wake up, I need you! Don't leave me alone in the dark! I can save us both, just look at me one last time!"

Vex did not stir. Pulling her close, Varka wept into her hair as the rain returned like a shower of stones. He gripped her limp form, holding onto the Ecstasy for what was left of his life. Weak beyond measure, Varka held onto life with quickly ebbing conviction. Time lost all meaning, as his existence became one endless moment of suffering beyond endurance. Wave after wave broke over the deck, crashing into them like an avalanche of ice. Varka held on even after exhaustion pulled him into an empty sleep.

Lightning cracked the sky open. Varka scrambled about with his frozen hands, but she was nowhere to be found. Another wave charged into him, filling his mouth and nose with ice and salt. Lightning flashed once more, and Varka beheld the outline of a woman crawling away from him.

• • • •

An aching pain woke Varka from his slumber. The broken decking had made for the worst night's sleep he'd ever had, but at least he hadn't rolled overboard. He stretched and yawned, amazed that he was still alive. A giddy laughter stole through him as he noticed the storm seemed to be subsiding. The angry clouds thinned, cracking apart as Oberon's opalescent glow poured through. Varka rose to his feet and welcomed the new day with arms wide open, filling his lungs with the calm ocean air. A hint of hyacinth crept through the air. It was an oddly familiar aroma, stirring vague memories and emotions. Perhaps a cask of wine had broken in the storm's rocking.

Shaking the sleep from his eyes, Varka took inventory of himself, patting his hands all over to check for wounds. His body was whole, and to his utter astonishment so was the cypher. The fragile orb had somehow survived the thrashing of the squall. Varka tossed the orb into the air with a flick of Wisdom, hovering it before his lips and kissing it. He wished he had more to show off from his battle with the Cold Crow, but for now this little orb would be his prize. Varka pocketed the cloudy egg, wondering why he hadn't perused its contents sooner. He was probably too caught up with trying to captain and crew the Ecstasy by himself. It was no easy task, being the sole member of the ship.

He managed the flimsy decking with careful steps, looking for the door that would lead him below deck. He approached the side of the Ecstasy, dismayed at how deep the hull had sunk. The lower decks were entirely submerged. Growling, he kicked at a loose plank, sending it skipping across the deck, where it collided with something solid.

Varka gasped. By some impossible miracle a lifeboat had survived the storm. He sailed across the deck with a burst of Wisdom, landing on all fours inside the lifeboat. The tiny vessel was stocked with enough food and fresh water to last him for weeks. If only he'd checked the little boat sooner! Varka threw his head back and cried to the stars, praising Oberon. His luck had finally returned.

THE END

If you enjoyed your journey to Aeneria and want to help make it a real place, please take a moment and give this book an honest review.

For all Hate mail and love letters:
www.AeneriaIsComing.com/contact/

FROM THE WORLD OF AENERIA

From the Author

Greetings Traveler!

I've been writing sporadically for most of my life. However, it wasn't until January 2016 that I began to take it seriously thanks to one of my closest friends. While I'd like to be writing full-time, I (like most independent authors) have a day job, which is a logistician position in the National Guard. I joined in 2005, deployed twice, and have been active duty since 2012. The military lifestyle has had a tremendous impact on my life, filling it with more ups and downs than I can keep track of, as well as some lifelong friends.

My days are spent at a desk or bumbling around in a humongous truck. After work I get myself to a gym and do battle with my inner fat kid for a couple of hours, then rush home and hopefully start writing before 8 pm. I nurture a love for performance arts, especially plays and local stand-up. During summers I don't ride my motorcycle nearly enough, and the same goes for my snowboard during the winters. At least once a year I'll go abroad, usually your typical over-indulgent Caribbean cruise, though recently I spent a week in France, where I had the privilege of officiating at a wedding for two dear friends.

The stories I enjoy the most usually leave me shaken for a few days, not because I'm a glutton for masochism, but because they resonate with the wounded parts of me that I wouldn't ordinarily take notice of. With a somewhat busy lifestyle where stoicism has become my go-to survival tool, I need those stories that derail me from my daily grind, that kick me in the gut and make me feel something.

As of writing this I'm 30 years old and live in Manchester, New Hampshire.

-Joe